FOR THE Love of Tom

MICHAEL KEENE

authorHOUSE®

AuthorHouse™ UK
1663 Liberty Drive
Bloomington, IN 47403 USA
www.authorhouse.co.uk
Phone: 0800.197.4150

Published by AuthorHouse   02/24/2015

ISBN: 978-1-4969-9865-1 (sc)
ISBN: 978-1-4969-9864-4 (hc)
ISBN: 978-1-4969-9866-8 (e)

CHAPTER 1

The war had been over for just six months. Life was gradually getting back to normal again in Purr, the sleepy village near Cambridge. The war had not really affected village life apart from the absence of young men that had left to fight abroad in 1914.

Bryan looked out of the bus window as it approached the edge of the county. Things appeared to be just the same, he thought. The countryside was flat, yet the green fields and low hedges were inviting him home again. It was a complete contrast to the damp water filled trenches he had been surviving in for what had seemed eternity. Trenches where even when you dared to raise your head over the top, it only depressed you with the view of dark dank mud filled fields and leafless looking trees wherever he had looked. It was good to be home again. People, on seeing him still in his army uniform and carrying his kitbag on his weary shoulders, smiled and welcomed him home even though they had never known him before. As he had climbed aboard the old bus, the money he had offered for his fare home was handed back to him with a smile of gratitude. The journey was taking over two hours, and he spent part of this trying to keep awake to look at the passing scenery he had missed so much over the past four years. At his journeys end a passenger awakened him with a gentle shaking of his shoulder. He looked up and thanked the old lady. He struggled off the bus with his kitbag and stood alone and slightly nervous on the kerbside. Everything seemed so peaceful and bright in the village-square. He was longing to see his mother's face as he stood on the doorstep of the family cottage once more. The long walk along the country lane seemed nothing now to him, as he had marched for days on end through mud filled ruts in the roads in Northern France for the past four years. He had written to his mother from the field hospital telling her of his return home, but he hadn't been sure at the time as to what day he would be released from having treatment for a minor injury to his leg. He took in a deep breath of country air. It felt so good in his lungs after all the smog like smoke of the battlefields he had suffered. For a moment he felt quite refreshed and free of his depression he had been suffering. Then, flashes of those last few days in the trenches flooded back into his head. He had to stop and sit down for a moment on the grass verge to collect himself. His pocket would not undo quick enough as he fumbled nervously for his weather beaten wallet. He opened it a stared at the dog-eared photo of Tom. Tears started to appear in the corners of his eyes as he touched the picture with his fingers and ran them across the good looks of his friend. If only he could feel the real flesh of Tom's face against his fingers. The last he had heard of him was when his corporal had sat at the side of his field hospital bed with the news that Tom had been taken from the trenches and transported back home by boat. The sound of a car coming down the lane broke his thoughts. He hurriedly put his wallet away and stood up, for the lane was only narrow. The car appeared around the bend in the lane. At first Bryan thought it was not going to stop, but just a few yards past him the brakes were applied. The driver's head appeared out of the car window. It wasn't anyone he knew. The woman was quite elderly.

'Can I offer you a lift?'

'Thank you.'

Bryan picked up his bag in his arms and hurried towards the car.

'I only live up the road about a mile, but a lift would be welcome.'

'A mile is a mile,' the woman said. 'Climb in.'

He placed his kitbag on the back seat, and then eased his way inside the small Austin car. The woman looked at him with penetrating but friendly eyes.

'I'm Doris Wetherby. You are?'

'Bryan Dobson.'

'Not Edna's son?'

'One of the same.'

'Oh my God. She will be pleased to see you. It's been a long war.'

Bryan smiled at her words. If only she knew. But then did anyone that hadn't gone to war know either?

'She, I mean Edna, talks about you at every WI meeting. Oh she will be pleased to see you again. 'Didn't you get wounded?' she asked, looking him up and down.

'Yes. But it's healed up well thank you.'

'Well here we are then. Didn't take long in the car, did it.'

Bryan thanked her and watched as the car disappeared out of sight down the lane. He stood there for a moment taking in deep breaths. He was going into an emotional situation again, and he wasn't quite sure if he could handle it. Placing his kitbag down on the front doorstep, he knocked on the door, then dashed to hide himself behind one of the many rosebushes at the corner of the cottage. He waited. Slowly the door was opened and he could hear her voice. It sounded much weaker than he remembered it.

'Oh my goodness. Who's there?' she called out. 'What on earth goes on? Oh it can't be surely? Bryan. Is that you?'

He poked his head around the rosebush, then appeared before her with open arms. He felt his mother's legs give way under her as they embraced on the doorstep.

'Thank God you are home safely. Let me look at you,' his mother cried.

'How have you been mum?'

'Don't worry about me. Let me look at you.'

'Are you alright?' he said, gently letting his hold on her go.

His mother stood back from him with one hand on the door frame and the other on his arm to steady herself.

'When did you last eat?'

'This morning at breakfast.'

'Come on in and sit down you poor boy. Listen to me - I mean - man.'

As they entered the cottage, it seemed much smaller than he had remembered. The sitting room was cosy and appeared quite dim with just small windows to let in light.

Once into the kitchen, he started to feel secure again with life, for this is the room where the family had sat down together mostly. This would never be the same now that his father had passed away. Joyce, his eldest sister, was married now and was living in Norfolk. His little sister Tina was away working as a nurse in Bristol. This had left his mother living on her own. She looked much older since he last saw her. But then, four years was a long time. He sat down at the large wooden table that had been scrubbed daily since he was a small boy. Nothing had changed in the room.

'I expect you would like a bath?' his mother suddenly said, breaking the silence.

'Yes I would.'

'I'll run it for you. Let me put the kettle on the stove first.'

There was an awkward sort of silence between them. His mother busied herself trying to avoid asking about the war. Each time she past him her hand reached out to touch him as if to check that he was real. He could hear her up in the bathroom as the tin kettle began to rock itself as it boiled. He got up from his chair to make the tea. It was as if he had never been away as he reached into the cupboard for the tin of tea, then reach up to another shelf for two mugs. Nothing had changed. Everything was still in the same place. Mother lived by her routines. He looked up at the family photographs in frames standing in line along the mantle piece over the kitchen range. Reaching up, he took hold of his father's picture. He had been a lovely man.

'I'm home dad,' he found himself saying.

'The water's running for your bath. And I've put your clean clothes out on your bed.'

'Mum. I could have done that. I was only injured in the leg.'

'Let me see it. Was it bad?'

'I'll show you it when I've had my bath. Tea first though. I've made it in the pot.'

They sat down at the table as his mother began to pour the tea. He looked at her. Nothing had changed for her. Still wearing her apron over her pure white cotton blouse and dark blue skirt. They smiled at each other. It was like old times again.

The next half an hour was filled with answering her questions about his war, and his dashing upstairs to check the bath water. He found it difficult in getting round her questions. If he had told her half of the truth about the war in the trenches, he knew she would not sleep in her bed for nights worrying about him. Anyway, he didn't want to relive his nightmares either. As he slowly eased himself into the steaming bath water, his body began to relax for the first time in months. His thoughts went back to the scene of his last bath. It had been in a tin bath that he and his mates had found outside a derelict farmhouse. They had lit a fire in the yard after finding pots and kettles to fill with water. There were only a few inches of water in the bath when it came to his turn to share it. He could still hear the shouts of his mates in his head as each one was seen to strip and jump into the bath in turn. He had been lucky as by the time it became his turn, more hot water had been boiled and tipped into his bath. It had been bloody cold when he had to get out and pull on his uniform over his wet body. They had lived like animals once back in the trenches. He had, like most, been so scared at times that he had just prayed for a bomb to fall and take his life. It was under one fierce attack that he found himself in the arms of the soldier next to him. As explosion after explosion made them duck their heads into their chests with fear, he remembers the slight sense of relief in being supported by another comrade. Once the last of the explosions had subsided, he remembered looking and smiling at this soldier in his arms. For a moment they looked at each other almost ashamed that they had reacted like they had. They introduced themselves. That was how he had first come to meet Tom. There was an instant chemistry between them. And from that moment on, they had remained good friends. It was that terrible night when without warning, a shell made a direct hit within a few yards of where Tom and himself had been crouching down trying to keep warm. The explosion threw them apart. He had blacked out. As he came around, a medic behind the lines was treating him. His first thoughts were for Tom. He couldn't find anyone that could tell him of Tom's fate. It was not until a few days later that the visiting corporal informed him that Tom had been shipped home. His mother's voice calling him from downstairs that snapped him out of his thoughts.

'I have a meal ready to put on the table for you. Will you be long?'

'No mum. I'm coming down. Give me a moment.'

He climbed out of the bath and started dying himself with the towel that had been hanging on the hook on the door. He shivered a little. He had stayed in the bath too long and the water was getting cold. But it was the first real bath he had had for weeks. He picked up his uniform clothes off the floor and made a pile of them in the corner of the bathroom. They were not fit to be worn any more, and he didn't want anything to do with them. He entered his bedroom and looked around. Nothing had changed as far as he could remember. He stopped to look at himself in the wardrobe mirror. He was thin now as against the fit athletic frame he used to have before going to war. He hadn't shaved for a couple of days, so that didn't help his gaunt looks. He pulled on fresh smelling clothes that his mother had laid out on his bed. He smiled at her old fashion ways of being a mum. She had even placed his full-length striped night-gown out onto his pillow. He couldn't remember the last time he had worn one of those. The flannelette shirt he pulled over his head felt so soft to his body, and as for clean underpants, God, what a luxury. Pulling on his grey flannel trousers with braces snapping over his shoulders, he was ready to face his mother again. As he combed his hair into place, with a side parting, the smell of home cooking drifted upstairs. He hadn't eaten good food for ages. The food in the hospital had not been that inviting. He hurried downstairs to join his mother who was just placing the plates down on the table. He cuddled her around her waist from behind. She gave a flick of her tea towel in her hand.

'Give over,' she said.

He sat in the wooden high-backed chair his father used to sit in at the table. His mother looked on with approval. The kitchen was warm and inviting at the best of times, but to him, this was what being home was all about. They eat and talked through the meal of lamb cutlets and potatoes and greens, and every now and again, he would take a swig of the stout from his father's drinking tankard. His mother wanted to know about the war, but he avoided her questions by asking her about how people had got on the home front. A couple of hours had passed away at the table before he was suddenly aware that his mother was shaking him gently on his shoulder. He opened his eyes and shook his head.

'What is the time? I must have drifted off to sleep.'

'Get you to bed. You are just like your father used to be, eat the meal, drink the beer, then fall asleep in his chair to get out of washing up,' she laughed. 'Come on. Bed for you and you can sleep in as long as you like my darling.'

'How long have I been asleep here?'

'Well it's nearly ten o'clock.'

He yawned and stretched his arms high above his head. His body ached through having slept in his chair. His mother smiled at him.

'It's good to have you home safe and sound, even if you do go to sleep on me.'

'I'm sorry mum. Did I snore?'

'No, but you were dreaming I think. It must have been terrible for you in those trenches. Terrible, terrible times we live in. Such a waste of young life.'

As she spoke, she moved around the table and placed her arms around him as he tried to get up from his chair. She pulled his head gently backwards and pressed it into her bosom and with her hands she traced his features with her fingers. He raised his head upwards. There were tears in her eyes. He buried his head back into her bosoms again and cried unashamed to be seen or heard. They stayed like that for ages without a word being spoken, both hanging on to the moment in silent prayer. Upstairs in his room, he pulled back the candlewick cover on his bed and climbed in between the clean white sheets without bothering with wearing his nightshirt. His head hardly touched his pillow before he was asleep. The dreams never eased up on him though. He had only been asleep a few hours when he sat bolt upright in bed, with perspiration running like a river down his body. The light went on, and his mother was kneeling across his bed to comfort him as he sat there with head in hands. 'Oh God, will they never go away,' he cried.

'You are safe now son,' his mother said, trying to console him as she placed her hands on his shoulders. 'Was it a bad dream? Do you want to talk about it?'

'No mum. I just want it to go away.'

'You were calling out aloud for Tom. Who's Tom?'

He opened his eyes and looked at his mother with questioning eyes. His face was white with panic now and his hair lay lank with perspiration.

'What was I saying about Tom?'

'Oh something about - Hold me tight - and - where is he?'

'Did I say anything else?'

'It was a jumble of words, I couldn't make out what you were saying really. Anyway, try and rest now.'

His mother eased him back onto his pillow, took a last look at him, then turned the light off. He lay there, his head still thumping and full of weird flashes of the past four years running through it. As he started to drift off to sleep again, his thoughts were with Tom. He would have to try and make contact with him in the morning. But where would he start to find out of his whereabouts?

CHAPTER 2

The sound of cups and saucers clinking together made him jump in bed. He raised his body slightly on the alert still. Then his mind cleared, he was home in bed again.

'Thought you could do with a good cup of tea and some toast. It's nearly two o'clock, not that that's a problem. Do you want the curtains drawn?'

'No thanks mum, I just want to keep my eyes closed for a little longer.'

'Well don't let your tea get cold. How are you feeling now?'

'Better for the sleep. Sorry about last night.'

'You scared me a little.'

He waited for her to leave his room before he made an attempt to sit up. He reached for his tea and sipped it. The cup felt so dainty after his usual enamel mug of vile tea that was infrequently handed out in the trenches. That nightmare had been so draining and felt so real. His thoughts were for Tom. Today he had to try and trace him. All he knew about him was that he lived in Thetford with his parents. He had an address, but there was no telephone number. They had talked about their lives before being drafted into the army, and like himself, Tom had lived a simple life in his village. He could write and invite himself up to see him. Yes, that was the best way to make contact. Maybe Tom might try and find him. They had gone through a lot together and there had been times that without each other's support he was sure that they might not have survived those days and nights in the mud filled trenches. His mother calling him to come downstairs as she had prepared a meal for him broke his thoughts He stood at his bedroom window looking out into the meadows beyond the garden. It looked so peaceful and calm. It was a warm summer's day, and memories of swimming in the river that ran through the meadow made him feel excited about being home again. Maybe the calm of the village he lived in would help erase the memories and horrors of the war. Maybe he could once again become sane in a troubled world. He pulled on his trousers. It was too warm to wear his flannelette shirt, so with his braces snapped over his shoulders, he made his way downstairs.

'Good morning mum.'

'Are you feeling better this morning?' mum asked, looking at his lean body. My God, you need fattening up. Come on, get some food inside you.'

He ate a hearty late breakfast and drank two mugs of hot tea. His mother moved around the kitchen to keep herself busy. He was glad that she had not started asking questions again. He wandered out into the garden carrying his mug of tea. He could feel his mother's eyes on his back as he strolled down the pathway. The garden had changed. Where the flowerbeds had been now vegetables grew. It must have been a hard time for his mother in trying to survive what with food rationing and little money coming in. He took hold of one of the pea pods and popped it open. The taste of fresh peas from the pod brought back fond memories of his time in the garden with his father. He had loved to grow his own vegetables, but his mother had now extended the garden and grew almost every vegetable. He walked through the fruit trees where the fruit was nearly ready for picking. Once through the orchard his bare feet felt the dampness of the grass where the trees shaded it from the sun. He suddenly felt like running through the grass as he had done as a teenager, but he was far from feeling well to do that. Suddenly the garden ended and the meadows started. He looked back toward the cottage. He could hardly see it through the trees. He stood there for a moment with memories of past years flooding back to him. Growing up with two sisters had been informative years, for once through the meadows the river ran deep and clear. He hastened his pace to retrace those happy days where they had swum together nude and free without a care in the world. He could hear the gentle sound of the river now as it trickled it's way past the meadows. Brushing the hanging finger thin boughs of the willow tress apart, he stood there looking down into the clear waters again. For a moment he thought he could hear the laughter and shouts of his sisters upstream as they swung out into the river on the rope swing they had made. For a moment he almost felt tempted to strip off and swim his way back into the past. As he headed back towards the cottage, he promised himself that he would return to the river later that evening when the dusk set in. Suddenly he began to feel better in himself as he kicked his bare feet through the long grass. The remains of his tea were cold so he tipped it across the vegetables. The curtains in the kitchen window fluttered and his mother's head disappeared from view.

'The garden has changed mum. You have been busy.'

'Had to do something to keep me occupied and fed. I went up the road to Mrs Vine to use her phone. I have spoken to both your sisters. They are ever so pleased that you are back safe and well again. They send their love.'

'That's nice. Are they going to come and see us?'

'I'm sure they will as soon as they can, but their war hasn't finished yet.'

'It will be good to see them again. I expect they have got much older.'

His mother smiled.

'Have you got writing paper mum?'

'In the top drawer of the sideboard.'

He went out into the garden and sat at the wooden bench table under the apple trees in the shade and wrote to Tom. How should he write? What should he write?

> *Dear Tom,*
>
> *I arrived home yesterday and just had to write to you straight away. I only have your parent's address to write to, so I hope this finds you. I can only remember you being stretchered away before I passed out that terrible day. Nobody was able to tell me where they had taken you after the field hospital. I know they shipped you home.*

I have been out of my mind with worry as to how bad your injuries were.

I will keep this letter brief, and hope that you will write back. If you have a telephone, please give me your number. My mother hasn't a phone in the house but I can use a friend of hers phone. As you will see, I'm not very good at letter writing, and there are lots of things I would like to put in a letter, but for now I will keep it short.

Please write back as soon as possible as I would like to come up and see you. God, isn't it difficult in writing to a friend? I found it easy talking in the trenches. I miss you.

Very sincerely,

Bryan Dobson

He read the letter over and over again. There was so much he had wanted to write into the letter, but he had no idea if Tom felt the same way about him. He sat there at the table thinking on the letter and the emotional feelings that ran through his head at times. Was it that it was because they were in such dreadful situations that he felt an attachment to Tom? Why had he felt that way when they clung together as the shells blasted away all around them? He could remember feeling the warmth of Tom's breath on his cheeks as their heads rested together as they snatched a few chances to sleep slumped like that in the mud and rain soaked trenches. The way Tom would light up two cigarettes and take one from his lips and pass it to him. Where these signs that he had been over reacting to? Should he have signed off the letter in a more personal way? Oh God, how he wished he knew Tom's feelings right now. He folded the letter and slipped it into the envelope, licked the gummed edge and sealed it. His mother had been watching him from the kitchen window. As he returned and entered the kitchen she asked if she should post it for him as she was going to the local shops and post office. He watched her as she walked down the front path and through the gate.

He smiled at the way she was holding the letter in her hand and the way she kept looking at the address. His mother had only left for the shops less than ten minutes when there was a knock at the front door. He ran upstairs to pull on his shirt and ran back down again to see who it was. It was Mrs Vine from up the lane. She stood on the doorstep smiling at him as he finished tucking his shirt into the top of his trousers.

'Well -Well. How are you feeling?' she asked.

'A lot better now that I'm home Mrs Vine, thank you.'

'You have altered a lot. Much thinner than when you went away. Poor boy,' she added. 'Was it very bad out there?'

'Yes.'

'Dear me.'

'Would you like to come in? Mum has just gone into the village.'

'No really. I just popped down to tell you I have had a phone call from your sister.'

'Really. Which one?'

'Joyce. She asked me to tell your mother that they were both going to try and come down to see you next weekend. Isn't that nice?'

'How nice,' Bryan said.

'Well I'll be off. You take good care of yourself.'

He thanked her and watched as she made her way down the front path and out of the gate. He remembered her as the village gossip. But she was the only one they knew that had a phone in the village, so people kept in with her. He went out into the garden and removed his shirt again so as to sunbathe. He had no idea as to how long he had been asleep before sounds from the kitchen woke him up. His body ached as he stretched his arms above his head. He looked towards the kitchen where he could see his mother fussing around the sink and looking out of the window at him. She waved.

'Cup of tea?'

'Please, he called back.

He was tempted to go for a swim as the evening sun was still warm, but he thought that it best to go later in the evening. As he entered the kitchen he broke the news that his sisters were coming to visit at the weekend. Her face lit up.

'That would be nice with us all together again.'

CHAPTER 3

—∿∘⌒◦⌒⊙⌒◦⌒∿—

The sun was going down fast now but the evening was still so warm as he made his way through the long grass of the meadow and down to the river. He looked back over his shoulders at the lights of the cottage flickering through the trees in the distance. It had been years since he had swam in the river. He loved this time of the evening to take a swim. He had fond memories of playing in the water with his two sisters. They were carefree days. A smile crossed his face as he remembered the laughter and teasing that went on between them. But by growing up this way swimming naked together it had answered many of the questions about life. He remembered the teasing he went through when the signs of his dark pubic hairs started to appear, and hairs started to appear under his armpits. Then there was the time when Joyce first noticed that she was growing breasts. They were all sitting on the fallen willow tree that acted as a dam in the river when Joyce announced her new body with pride. They sat there staring at them, and he had had an erection to hide, which drew their attention away from Joyce. Then it was Tina's turn to sprout breasts, which made them all equal. The girls had asked him if he could produce another stiff one for them, but he couldn't.

He reached the spot where they used to strip off and swim up stream to the willow tree. Nothing had changed and the warm evening was just as he remembered it back in those happy days. He took his shoes shirt and trousers off and stood naked on the riverbank with his arms wrapped around him. God, this was what he had been missing. He gently eased himself into the flowing water. It felt cold at first, but as he pushed himself off into the depth of the midstream it felt so good with the water washing over him. The moonlight seemed to light up his path that headed him to the willow tree. He was a little out of condition swimming up stream and his breathing became harder, but he felt so free and secure now he was back doing the things he had done in his youth. He could see the tree ahead now and he seemed to glide through the water towards it. Grabbing hold of the tree trunk so as to stop himself drifting past it, he hauled himself up and sat with his legs dangling in the water. The tree was just as he had remembered it. He spread his hands along the trunk where his sisters had sat with him, and for a moment he could almost hear their chatter and laughter. Oh, what a bloody war it had been. What a waste of youthful years the past four years had been, for he had been snatched away to fight for his country when he was eighteen. He wondered though, if the war had not interrupted their lives, if they would still have been swimming together now. He let his body slip down into the water as he hung onto the trunk with his arms letting the rush of water caress his nakedness and wash away some of the horrors of war. He stayed there in the water with his head resting on his arms. The sadness and memories of his war suddenly overcame him and tears formed in his eyes. His sobbing could have been heard along the length of the tow-path, but there was nobody to hear him. He closed his eyes trying to eliminate the flashes of exploding shells in his mind. He clung tight onto the tree trunk as if he was with Tom again. God, would these memories ever go away? He swam over to the bank and started to walk back towards the spot where his clothes were. By the time he reached the spot, his body was almost dry. Dabbing the odd droplets of water off of his body with his flannel shirt, he then slipped on his trousers and headed back home. The lights from the cottage twinkled through the trees as he reached the garden. He felt calmer now, and secure in being home. His mother looked up from her knitting as he entered the kitchen.

'There's tea in the pot if you want one,' she said, eyeing him up and down as she spoke. She knew what he was going through, and knew that he wanted peace to be with himself. She would wait for the time when he wanted to pour out the horrors of war to her. She would be there for him. They talked a while about the coming weekend when they would be together as a family. He watched his mother's face and her glances up to the picture of his father sitting up on the mantelpiece as they spoke of their reunion. He held out his hand to hold hers. She smiled as she wiped away a tear with the back of her free hand.

'Get on with you. Get to bed and get some rest,' she said, shaking his hand free.

In bed that night his dreams turned to nightmares again. With his body wet with fear as he lay there with his head buried in his pillow sobbing into it so as not to disturb his mother again. For a moment he could feel the comforting hand of Tom's around his shoulder. He placed his own hand there to touch it, but it wasn't there. If only it were. In the morning when the sunlight streamed through his bedroom window, he lay there exhausted once again. His army doctor had told him that there would be nights like the ones he was experiencing now, but he never said how long they might go on for. If this was to be his life, then what was the point of living? It would have been better to have died alongside Tom in the trenches. He sat up in bed. He suddenly felt cold even though he was sitting in sunlight. Thoughts like this had to be dismissed from his head, and he had to try and fill his head with good thoughts such as seeing his sisters again at the weekend. As he sat there letting good thoughts enter his head; he wondered how his letter was going to be received by Tom. Did Tom have the same feelings for him, or was he reading too much into the friendship and bonding that they had had in the front line trenches.

There was an air of excitement in the cottage as he awaited the arrival of his two sisters. His mother busied herself with washing and re-washing cups and mugs in a nervous state. Bryan had stood at her side waiting to dry them with his tea towel. They both laughed as he reminded her that he had already dried the dishes she was washing again. The kitchen clock seemed to be getting slower as they waited the arrival. As time dragged on the excitement was almost too much for his mother as they heard the sound of a car engine drawing up outside the cottage. It was the local taxi.'

'Here they are. They are here,' she called up to him.

He leaned out of the upstairs window to watch as his mother ran down the garden path to the gate. For a moment he felt suddenly nervous. The sound of people had made him feel insecure since leaving the hospital. The past few days had had a calming effect on him, but now he was going to be the centre of conversation, he felt nervous again. He watched as his mother flung her arms around his two sisters to greet them as they climbed out of the taxi. He half wanted to go down and join them, but he wanted his mother to enjoy the reunion. Joyce seemed much older than he had expected to be as she stood back waiting for her turn to be greeted by mum. She had put on a little weight and was more rounded. From where he was viewing the scene below, Joyce looked tired.

When Tina had been released from mum's clutches he could see that she was just the same as he last saw her. Tina looked up at the window and blew a kiss up to him. She called out something, but he missed what it was as he began to make his way downstairs to the greeting party. His heart was in his mouth, and he felt nervous all of a sudden. It had been four years now since seeing his sisters. How would he react to their questions about the war?

Tina and his mum were still embracing each other, so he held out his arms towards Joyce. She hugged and kissed him taking all his breath out of his body.

'Let me look at you,' she said, releasing him for a moment and holding him at arm's length. 'God it's good to see you in one piece. How much weight have you lost? Never mind, a few weeks with mum's food inside you and you'll look more like the brother that went off to fight for his country.'

'You haven't changed a bit,' he replied, embracing her again in his arms. It was good to have physical contact with someone again. Oh how he wished he had Tom in his arms right now. He felt emotions running through his body and tears forming in the corner of his eyes. He gave a sniff.

Joyce gave a knowing pat of her hand on his back.

'Let me get at him,' Tina was heard to be saying. 'Oh you poor thing. It must have been terrible for you. Come here and kiss me so I know you are real.'

Once again he was enveloped in family reunion. Memories flooded through his head of past years of growing up together. If only those years could be repeated. Growing up in the company of two girls in the rather remote countryside must have had some kind of influence on his sexuality. This had troubled him, yet the only feelings he had experienced were with the comforting contacts with Tom in the trenches. He wondered how Tom had received his letter. If they met up again, would Tom have the same feelings for him now, or was it that he had read the wrong message about Tom's feelings for him? When would he get a return letter? Maybe Tom would not write back.

Tea in the garden under the shade of the apple trees made him feel nervous for some reason. Although the conversation did not always involve his wartime experiences, he could feel his sister's eyes searching him as he sat there in his deckchair. He had no idea how long he had been asleep, but he suddenly began to hear the buzz of conversation as he came out of his slumbers. He partly opened his eyes. His mother and sisters were deep in conversation. Their voices were in a hush, and he could see their glances at him sitting there, body slumped and arms folded.

'Sorry. I must have dozed off,' he said, as he sat up and rubbed his hands over his face.

'Don't you worry my pet, you sleep as much as you want,' his mother said. ' You haven't drunk your tea or eaten your cake.'

'How long have I been asleep?'

'Not long,' Tina replied. 'I'll make another pot of tea.'

He watched her make her way down the lawn towards the cottage. It brought memories of the past racing back to him. Tina was his favourite sister. He had always got on with her better than Joyce. Maybe it was that she was the elder one of the two. He looked across at her. The years had not been kind to her. Maybe over the weekend she would unload her troubles to them all. As the evening drew on, it was still very warm. They tried to sit indoors in the kitchen as they used to in the past, but it was too hot for that. He suddenly felt like taking a swim to cool off. The three women were full of women talk. He excused himself from the lawn where they were all sitting.

'I just want to take a walk,' he said suddenly.

The conversation died for a moment. As he walked through the garden and into the meadow, he could hear them laughing together again. He was pleased for his mother. It must have been hard for her living alone through the war. The sound of the river flowing sounded peaceful as he stood there on the riverbank. It was a good feeling having removed his clothing and easing his body into the cool water. Ducking his head under the water seemed to take him into another world of silence. He swam towards the fallen tree trunk, dipping his head under the surface every now and again to help relax his mind from the pressures of the past four years. As he rounded the bend he could see the willow tree with its fallen trunk. The sight of this added to his sense of security. Dipping his head under the water once again, and as he surfaced again he reached out and took hold of the trunk. With arms resting over the trunk for a while, his thoughts went back to those days when he and his sisters used to play together there. Hauling himself up onto the trunk he sat there picturing scenes of the past. It had all been so natural in the way they had learned about each other's bodies as they grew up over the years. Their parents had been the first to introduce them to the river and teach them to swim in the shallows. Then as they grew up they were allowed to venture down to the river alone to play. He remembered the day when they played the game of *truth or dare*. He decided to take a *dare*. Being only seven at the time he had thought it funny when the dare was to take his swimming costume off and go in swimming. He had struggled around on one foot in an attempt to remove his costume in a hurry so as to get into the water as fast as he could. The girls had laughed at his antics and the way they had fallen into the water in an ungainly fashion. They had shouted out aloud for him to climb out of the water and do it all again. He did. Soon they were all in the water swimming around naked. Since that time they had never bothered with costumes. And since then, they had never had to believe the smutty school kids stories. They had been informative days. He wondered what the kids got up to now. The tree trunk in the river had been their meeting place. At one time there had been a rope tied to another tree which they used as a swing. He looked around to see if there were any signs of the rope still there today. The years had worn it away. The sound of splashes in the water broke his thoughts. Someone was swimming his way. He squinted through the shadows that the sun and evening darkness conjured up. Nobody had ever been seen in their private play area before. He slipped his naked body down into the water for modest protection, and waited. To his delight and relief he could make out Tina's head bobbing up and down in the water as she swam towards him. He swam to meet her.

'I thought I'd find you here,' Tina said.

They met and trod water as they greeted each other. It was just like old times again.

'I had to get away for a while,' he replied.

'Guess it must be hard for you. Was it very bad out there in the trenches?'

'I really don't want to talk about it if you don't mind.'

They swam together towards the tree trunk. He helped Tina up onto it, laughing at the way she needed help.

'I'm getting old,' she said.

'Me too. Give me a hand up.'

They sat there together in silence for a while with just the odd flutter of sunlight drifting through the willow trees as the evening drew to a close. He looked at Tina's body. She had put on a little weight, but looked better for it. He looked up at her face. She smiled.

'Go on, tell me I've put on weight,' she said.

'You look well on it,' he laughed.

'You've lost such a lot of weight.'

He looked down at his own body. If only she knew what it had been like.

'How's your nursing then?'

'Hard. But I enjoy the work.'

'Have you a man yet?'

'That's none of your business,' she smiled, but her eyes showed that she had.

'What's his name then?'

'Give over.'

'You sound like mum,' he joshed.

'Who's this Tom then that mum tells me about?'

'What did she tell you?' he asked, feeling suddenly embarrassed.

'Well she said that you called out for him in your sleep. Is he your friend?'

'We shared the horrors of the trenches together. I tell you Tina, I don't think I could have survived it without him. God it was awful,' he told her, tears started to form in his eyes.

Tina put her arm around his shoulders to comfort him. He laid his head on her shoulder and started to sob relentlessly. He felt her kiss the top of his head.

'Sorry,' he eventually said, sniffing back his tears and wiping his nose with the back of his hand.

'Don't be. Come on let's swim back, Tina suggested.

They eased themselves back into the water and began swimming. It was as if they had only been away for a short while as they both swam to the far bank, which they used to do, then they climbed out to walk the rest of the way back to their clothes. This way they would be dry enough to pull on their clothes again before they reached the cottage. They laughed at their return to teenage years again as they skipped around in the meadow trying to dress.

'Tell me about Tom. Is he nice?' Tina suddenly asked as they adjusted their clothing.

'Yes he is nice. I like him a lot. We got separated when a shell landed near us. He got sent home.

I've written to him, but I'm not sure if he is home yet or still in hospital.'

Sleep that night did not come easy. He had another nightmare and tried to muffle his cries into his pillow so as not to wake the others. As he sat up in bed with sweat rolling down his body, he found himself cradling his pillow with his arms and between his thighs. He had visions of Tom in his head, and he was suddenly aware that he had an erection on him. It had been ages since he had had one. He fell back onto the bed and his hand reached for his penis. God what was going on in his mind and body? He worked on himself with frantic actions, yet nothing happened. Why had he been excited about Tom in his dreams? But then, he hadn't been in the company of a woman for love for over five years. He lay there in bed with his frustrations pounding in his head. Sleep eventually overcame him and morning arrived. He waited until the bathroom became free, and stood there at the basin splashing cold water over his face and running his wet hands around his body to remove the sweat from his nightmare. He dressed and went downstairs to the smell of a cooked breakfast being prepared. His sisters greeted him with smiles and kisses. Mum was at the stove cooking eggs and bacon. She turned her head as he put his arms around her waist to greet her with a morning kiss. Suddenly he began to feel more relaxed than he had been for ages. The radio was playing music from the other side of the kitchen. He sat down to listen to it. It had been a while since he had listened to a radio.

'You had another bad night,' his mother suddenly said.

He nodded. It was one of those moments that a youth has when he suspects that his parents have knowledge of his private happenings. It was as if his mother had known that he had tried to masturbate in his bed last night. Guilt was a funny thing he thought. It concerned him that he had not got satisfaction or pleasure out of it though. Had that been taken away from him due to the stress of war?

'There you are, eat up,' his mother said, placing the breakfast in front of him. 'And stop your worrying. We want you back as the Bryan we all knew.'

'Oh no. Not quite like that,' Joyce giggled.

He sat there eating his breakfast and part listening to the chatter of his sisters and his mother while trying to listen to the radio in the background. As he sipped the last of his mug of tea, he suddenly wanted to be free of the chatter. He could feel the eyes of his sisters on his back as he wandered off into the garden. The sun was beginning to get warmer. It was nearly ten o'clock. He sat down on the wooden bench seat his father had made. Running his hand along the now smooth wood surface, his thoughts turned to his father. He had only known him up to his teen years. It came as a shock when he had died suddenly, for he had been the strength of the family, and a model father. His mother had always moaned about him being out there in his potting shed until it was time for bed. The weekends were the best when they all used to go off into the countryside for a picnic together.

He wandered down to the potting shed and tugged at the door which was warped with the weathered years. The wood had not been touched for years, maybe not since his father had last worked in there. He picked up the rusty old hand fork and held it in his hand for a moment. To think that the last time this had been touched was by his father. It sent a funny feeling through his body at the thought of that. He went to sit down on the wooden stool, but felt suddenly cold at the thought. Best leave the shed as his father had left it closing the door behind him. He wandered down the garden and into the meadows beyond. It was peaceful out there on his own. The grass was high. He pulled at one of the sheaths of grass and drew at the stem and placed it in his mouth. It tasted sweet as he sucked on it. Memories of his youth flooded back to him as he stood there looking down towards the river beyond. They had been happy days. If only those days could return.

Back in the cottage again he found his mother making sandwiches with his sisters. The old picnic basket rested open on the table and they were filling it with fruit and cakes just as he remembered.

'I thought we would head off into the fields and have a picnic today. The girls have to go back on the five o'clock train, so at least we can get some fresh air in their lungs before then,' she said.

'Is there anything I can do?' he asked.

'You can get a blanket from the cupboard in my bedroom. The tartan one we used to use. It might be right at the bottom.'

He opened his mother's bedroom door and went inside. It seemed strange being in the room where his parents used to sleep together. He smiled at the memory of the time he caught them making love under the sheets as he had burst in the room one summer's morning. His father had shouted at him to knock first before coming in. His mother had turned her face away from him in embarrassment, but his father remained on top of her. That was the first of his lessons on life. Much later his father had used that moment to explain how babies were made. At the time it had all been a mystery to him as a small boy. At the age of fourteen, he had been tempted to make love to a girl in the village. She was much older than he was. They had fumbled around in each others clothing and clashed teeth as they attempted to kiss, but when he found himself laying on top of her as he had seen his father do in bed that morning, it was all over in a second. The girl never spoke to him again, but he was sure that she had told almost every girl in the school about his failure. It was at the age of sixteen before he tried it again. This time it was with an older female known for her desire for the younger man. He remembered her giggles as he attempted to be manly in his actions. He had in his dreams seen himself as being masterful when it was time to have sex with a female. In reality he failed his dream. In his haste to prove his mature technic in sexual play his boldness became too much for her, and her giggles turned to crying. His attempts to have sex with females turned to failure until he was called up to fight in the war at eighteen. It was not a scene that he let enter his head too often. He had been drinking with his mates in uniform. They knew they were due to be shipped out to fight in the war the following day. The six of them shared the prostitute they had found. He had been fifth in turn urged on by the other four. She had been a hard face bitch and lay there taking him in as she continued smoking her cigarette as if he were not there. He had tried to arouse her with his forceful efforts, and for a moment he thought he had done so. But as he climaxed looking down at her plump naked body, he just wanted to make her regret her disgusting acts. She had remained unimpressed. He had felt sick after it was all over.

'Have you found that blanket yet?' he heard his mother call out from downstairs.

His head was snapped into gear again and his thoughts of the past faded as he searched in the cupboard for the blanket.

'Got it,' he called out, and hurried downstairs.

The four of them walked through fields of long grass until they found their favourite spot of past years of fun together. The sun was hot as they lazed around having eaten their sandwiches and drank lemonade together. They talked about their father and how they missed him. He watched his mother's face as they did so. She could be seen brushing back tears with the back of her hand trying not to be seen doing so. Tina talked about some of the stories from her work in the hospital. Nursing had its sad side as well, but she tried to avoid talking about that. Joyce talked about married life and her part time job in her village store. Bryan envied her having someone to share her life with. They also talked about the games they used to play. Mum spoke about their swimming in the river together. To this day she had no idea that they skinny dipped and just dunked their costumes in the river to make them appear to have been worn when swimming. They laughed at the way mum used to wash them under the tap and put them through the mangle, then hang them out on the wooden clotheshorse in the kitchen to dry for the next day. He looked at Tina and the way she had grown into a young woman. He wondered why she had not found a handsome young man to settle down and marry. Maybe she was so devoted to her nursing. His thoughts were interrupted as he listened to the conversation going on around him. Tina was heard to be suggesting that he should start getting out and about to find a nice young woman to settle down with and have a family. Joyce had been saying that he would have to find work again before that. They spoke as if he were not there. His mother came to the rescue by telling the two of them that he needed rest first of all, and that they had no idea of how troubled he was from the war front. He roused himself from his sleeping position as if he had not overheard them.

'More lemonade?' his mother asked him.

Later that afternoon there were emotional scenes as the clock ticked around for time to part. He waited outside the kitchen as his mother kissed and hugged his sister's farewell. As he walked them down the lane towards where the bus stopped, they almost walked in silence for they knew it was going to be a long time before they met up again. The bus arrived and they said their goodbyes. It was almost too emotional a time for him to handle. He waved to them as the bus went out of view around the bend of the road. Suddenly he felt alone. As he walked back to the cottage kicking the odd stone ahead of him, his thoughts went back to the conversation he was not intended to hear.

What was he going to do with his life now he was back from the war? They were right, he would have to seek work again. Maybe he could get his old job back at the farm again. As for finding a woman to settle down with, the thought of that made him feel even more insecure.

CHAPTER 4

———~w∘⊙∘⊙⊙∘∘w———

Two days had past since his sisters had visited the cottage and he was tired of sleeping under the shade of the apple tree in the garden. He had tried reading, yet found he could not concentrate long enough to enjoy the story. Gardening was a bore although it was helping to regain strength in his body. Standing at the front gate looking for who knows what down the lane was driving him crazy, so he just had to get out into the village and meet up with people again. After he'd showered and found out some of his old clothes that he used to wear, he stood in front of the mirror looking at the fit of his clothes on his now slim body. Depression was setting in rapidly now for the clothes almost clung onto him rather than fitting as they did. That meant he would have to go into town and buy some more if that were possible what with rationing. There was nothing for it; he would have to make do with what he had. As he opened the gate and closed it behind him, suddenly he felt insecure about taking those steps towards the village half a mile away. Taking a deep breath he started walking. He looked back at the cottage and was sure that he saw the curtains flutter from the upstairs bedroom window. Poor old mum, he thought, she worried about him a lot. His steps along the lane faltered at times as he tried to collect himself. Somehow his confidence had left him and he began to feel nervous about being alone. He forced himself to keep walking and the sight of the village brought yet another strange feeling running through his head. People, he wasn't ready to meet up with people. He had to find somewhere to sit down for a while. The pub, yes the pub. Pushing the saloon door open he made for the bar and rested on it with a grim determination not to let himself pass out. He could hear the barman's voice as if it were in a tunnel.

'What can I get you young man?'

He looked in the direction of the voice, but his vision was not clear.

'A pint of beer. Just a pint please,' he muttered.

'Are you alright son?'

'A pint please.'

He fumbled in his pockets for money and paid the barman as he was handed his beer. As he made his way across the bar the beer slurped over his hand and onto the bar floor. Crashing his way through the doors to get outside again, he sat down on the first bench seat he came across. He was sweating yet felt cold. Gulping at his beer seemed to revive him a little and his nerves seemed to calm down a little. He closed his eyes hoping that when he opened them all would be right again.

His heart was beating faster than normal. Then suddenly he felt a hand resting on his shoulder.

'Are you OK mate?' he heard a voice asking him.

He opened his eyes and look at the stranger that was concerning himself about him.

'Just feeling a bit rough thanks,' he replied looking up at a young man's face.

He felt the hand pat his shoulder again and then run down the length of his back. It was a friendly touch, one that he reacted to as the touches of Tom's used to do to him. He felt the bench seat move as the stranger sat down at his side.

'Can I help?' the stranger asked.

'I'll be fine in a minute. Just felt rough for a moment.'

'Haven't seen you around here before,'

'I live here, but I've been away in the war.'

'Shit. Is that a fact? Poor bastard'

Bryan looked at the young man as his vision cleared. He sipped at his beer and nodded.

'I'm Doug.'

'Bryan.'

There was a silence between them for a moment. Bryan looked at Doug and tried to judge his age. He must have been about eighteen he thought.

'Were you in the forces?' he asked Doug.

'Just missed out on it all. Wish I had gone though.'

'I don't think so. It was bloody hell. I'm trying to get myself together even now, and the wars been over for months.'

He felt Doug pat his shoulder again. There was something about the touch of his hand that was more that a touch of concern. Was this saying something more to him? He looked at Doug and they smiled at each other.

'There. The man can smile after all,' Doug said. 'Can I get you another beer?'

'No Thanks.'

There was a silence again. He had not felt this way since being with Tom. He turned to look at Doug more closely in an attempt to see any signs of him being gay. But then, why should he be doing that? Did that mean that he was? Doug had quite classic features with deep-set dark eyes and high cheekbones. He wore his hair short and neat and his complexion was clear. Doug's eyes never flinched at Bryan's searching eyes. He smiled to show the whiteness of his teeth.

'Look I've got to go soon,' Doug suddenly said. 'Are you going to be alright?'

'Yes. Thanks. I just felt a bit nervous about coming out and meeting people again. Can I buy you a drink some other time?'

'I don't think so. Well not for a while. You see, I'm leaving here for a while to find work.'

'Where?'

'London. I've got a chance of working with a printer friend down there.'

'When?'

'Next week,' Doug said, as he started to stand up to leave. 'Look you can buy me a beer tomorrow. I'll be around here about seven o'clock.'

With that, Doug patted him on his back and strolled off out of sight. He sat there looking in his direction; it was as if someone had walked out of his life for good. He knew that Doug's touches meant more than just someone being concerned. They had a deeper meaning, or was he just clutching at straws in hope that he had found a meaningful friend to relate to? Was it always going to be like this? He felt suddenly alone in the world with nobody to turn to. Having finished his beer, he started to walk through the village with his vision playing tricks with him. Someone spoke to him, but he never turned to look back as he forced himself to walk in a straight line. His mind was a whirl, and he became desperate to get home again. Somehow he reached the gate to the cottage. His mother greeted him with one of her knowing looks. She knew what he was going through.

'Tea, my dear?' she asked.

He nodded as he sank his body down into a chair.

'There's a letter there for you.'

'When did that come?' he asked excitedly.

'Just now while you were out.'

He stared at the envelope sitting there on the table propped up against the biscuit tin. His hand was shaking as he reached out for it. The postmark was not clear, but he was sure it was from Tom. He sat there for a moment staring at the letter. Slowly he began to open it to read.

> *My Dear Bryan,*
>
> *So good to hear from you. I had to reply as soon as your letter reached me. I have recovered well from that dreadful day, but have been out of my mind and worried about you as they had no bloody idea where you were or if you were alive. So you have no idea how pleased I was to get your letter. I'm not very good at letter writing as well, so I have got the telephone number But why don't you phone me [see my number at the top of this page] I would love to meet up with you again, maybe we could meet up soon I hope.*
>
> *Sincerely,*
>
> *Tom.*

He sat there holding the letter in his hand not quite believing that Tom had replied. He read the letter again, then sat back in his chair feeling relieved that he had not lost touch with Tom.

'Who's the letter from?' his mother asked.

'Tom. He wants me to phone him. Do you think Mrs Vine would let me use her phone?'

'I'm sure she wouldn't mind. Why don't you walk down and see her.'

He read the letter again, and then replacing it back into the envelope he got up from the table and left the kitchen. As he walked towards Mrs Vine's cottage, which was at the other end of the lane, he tapped the envelope against his lips in thought. For a moment he stood at her front gate hesitating as to how he should put it to her that he wanted to speak to a friend. What if she stood there listening to his conversation? He closed the gate behind him and walked tentatively up to the front door. Taking a deep breath, he knocked at the front door and waited. Mrs Vine soon opened it. She stood there staring at him for a second before speaking.

'You're young Bryan, aren't you?'

'Yes. Sorry to disturb you, but is it alright if I use your phone?'

'Of cause it is my dear. Come on in. Oh, you poor boy,' she said, standing aside to let him into the hallway. 'What a terrible war it was for you,' she continued. Your mother, bless her, told me all about it. Must have been terrible. Are you all right now?'

'I'm fine, thanks. It's just that a friend from the army is trying to contact me.'

'Go on then. There's the phone. Help yourself. I'll shut myself in the kitchen so as you can be private. Just pick up the phone and the operator will ask you for the number.

He waited for the kitchen door to be closed, then picking up the phone he waited nervously for the operator to answer. When she did, his throat had dried up on him. He coughed, then apologised.

41

He waited while the number rang out. The palms of his hand were sweaty.

'Hello.'

It was a woman's voice at the other end of the phone.

'Hello. I would like to speak to Tom please.'

'Who's calling?'

'It's Doug.'

He waited as he heard Tom's name being called to the phone. He suddenly felt more nervous than usual. What should he say? He heard the sound of a door being opened. He glanced at the kitchen door, but it was still closed. Then he was suddenly aware that someone was coming down the stairs. He turned and looked. To his surprise it was Doug that he had met earlier. Their eyes met as they looked at each other in surprise. He could hear the voice of Tom on the other end of the phone. Doug put his finger to his lips as he shuffled down the hall and into the kitchen. He had touched him on the shoulder as he had passed him in a friendly manner.

'Hello, Hello,'came Tom's voice down the phone.

'Hello Tom. Just a moment,' he said, trying to collect himself from the surprise of seeing Doug in the house. 'How are you?'

'Nice to hear from you. Christ, I thought I'd lost contact with you. How are you?'

'I'm fine now, but how are you?'

He heard a chuckle down the phone.

'I could be better. But just glad to be alive.'

'Me too. Tell me what happened to you?'

'Do you know, I really don't remember too much about it after the bang. What about you?'

'I just remember crouching with you as they shelled us, then nothing until I was in hospital.'

'Where did they take you?' Tom asked.

'Oh, it was the field hospital behind the lines. Then I was sent home to a hospital for treatment. It's my head that wants sorting out...I dream about it all the time.'

'Me too. Look, can't we meet up somewhere? I'd like that, Tom said.'

'You could come down here in Cambridge and stay for a while. That would be great.'

'When?'

'When you feel you can make it.'

Bryan hesitated for a moment. Was that the kitchen door started opening? He turned his head slowly in the direction of the kitchen, but the door was only just slightly ajar. Maybe he was imagining it. Tom could be heard down the phone asking if all was all right.

'Sorry. It's just that I'm on someone else's phone, and I can't say too much just now.'

'So when can we meet up?' Tom asked.

'How about you come down next weekend and stay for the week?'

'That sounds good. Where do I catch the train to?'

As it wasn't private enough to talk any further, the arrangements where left that he would meet Tom at the station at the nearest to mid-day train to arrive the following Saturday. Placing the phone down he knocked on the kitchen door. It opened almost immediately.

'Thank you for letting me use the phone Mrs Vine,' he said, peering past her and into the kitchen to see if Doug was still there.

'You are welcome,' came her reply. ' I'll see you out.'

'I'll do that mum,' Doug called out, and eased his way through the kitchen door past his mother.

Bryan felt Doug's hand on his shoulder as they headed for the front door.

'This is weird. Fancy seeing you again so soon. How are you now?'

'Fine thank you. I didn't know you lived here.'

'Not for much longer,' Doug replied.

'Will you miss the village?'

'I will now I've met you,' Doug smiled as he patted Bryan on his back again. 'But it was pretty dead in the village up till now.'

Bryan was lost for something to say. They seemed to linger in the doorway for a while. And he could sense the chemistry between them, yet neither was able to respond.

He waved back at Doug as he closed the front gate. There was a sadness that ran through his body. If only they had met up earlier. Life played tricks on people like them, he thought. He stopped for a moment in the lane and reflected on his thoughts as they ran through his head. *People like them!*

What was this sudden attraction to another man? Was it sudden, or had he always been attracted to his own sex but never accepted it? For a moment he wanted to turn and go back to see Doug again. But that was not going to prove anything, for Doug was going away to London. He suddenly felt tense again. Instead of walking back to the cottage, he headed along the riverbank. Although he had never ever seen anyone walking along this part of the river, he suddenly felt insecure as he removed his shirt and socks and shoes. For the first time for many months now he felt pressure in side his trousers. His body began to shake as he realised that he was getting an erection. He couldn't remember the last time he had felt like this. Pulling down his trousers hurriedly, he eased his naked body down into the cool waters of the river and struck out swimming towards the tree again. There was an urgency about his strokes now. He felt excited and free again. He reached out for the tree and clung onto it. Pulling himself up onto the trunk of the tree, he spread himself out on his back as his erection returned. As he relaxed there he began to feel signs of a natural erection arising. Oh God what had the effects of the war done to him. It had been ages since he had felt like this, and he was not sure that he was going to be able to raise himself to the dizzy heights that he used to be able to in past years. The sun was now streaming through the trees and played patterns on his nakedness. He flung his head backwards and arched his back as he pleasured himself. He muffled his attempts to call out at his revived sexual pleasure as he watched the rewards erupt and drift into the river. As he lay there in flaccid state, he had visions of Tom running through his head. He smiled to himself as he watched the flowing river water drift his love juices away down stream, for life had returned into his body again, and he suddenly felt alive again.

He felt good as he walked along the tow-path to collect his clothes. He smiled to himself as he reached the spot and started to pull his shirt over his head, for this was the spot that had seen the hurried piles of clothes of his two sisters and himself since the happier days of their youth. As he entered the meadow and headed for the kitchen garden of the cottage, he could see his mother collecting the washing from the clothesline. She turned and waved as he approached.

'Hello darling. Did you get through to your friend?'

'Yes I did. It was good speaking to him again.'

'Has he recovered from his stay in hospital?'

'Yes I think so. I have invited him to come and spend a few days together with me. Is that all right with you? Sorry I should have asked first.'

'That would be nice for you. When is he coming?'

'Next weekend. Is that too early for you to get prepared for him?'

'I'll have to air the bed in the spare room. A few hot water bottles will do that. The room hasn't been used for years. I'll have to make some stews and get some more eggs from the farm.'

He placed his arms around her portly body and gave her a squeeze. Suddenly the world seemed a brighter place to be in. He felt her kiss him on the cheek as she removed his arms from around her.

'Go on with you. I've got a lot to get ready before the weekend,' she said, as she bent to gather up the washing in the old basket that had seen better days.

'Let me do that,' he said.

'Get on with you. I've done this for years on my own, so I'm not about to ask for help,' she said, as she headed back towards the cottage.

He smiled as he watched her plump backside wobble with her every stride. It must have been tough for her being on her own during the war, he thought. But there was a renewed spring in her step now. Maybe the coming visit of Tom would do them both some good.

CHAPTER 5

The week seemed to drag. It was a mixture of relief that he had broken through the emotional barrier and fear that he had lost his sexual desire forever. His nights in bed were becoming less fearful of nightmares, and that the stirring in his loins were becoming more frequent. Maybe it was the thought of Tom's visit that made him this way. Then he started to worry about other issues. What if Tom rejected his advances? What if Tom was not gay at all? Maybe he had misinterpreted Tom's protective holds as the shells burst around them in the trenches? But then Tom had on one occasion placed the side of his face against his, and they stayed like this for a while. Maybe he was worrying too much? His mother had given the cottage a spring clean, prepared food in advance, and the spare bedroom had been given extra attention too. If only his mother knew how much he wanted to have Tom share his room with him. Maybe it was all for the good anyway. Maybe he was destined to live his life out without being able to share a desired love of another man.

Saturday came around at long last. It would take him less than an hour to walk to the station, and it was only nine o'clock. He sat around trying to read a book, but his concentration failed him. As he looked out of his bedroom window across the meadow, he could picture walking through the long grass with Tom at his side. He imagined how it would be to have that first touch as they lay amongst the sweet smelling grass. Maybe he could tempt Tom to swim in the river with him. That would be heavenly. What would Tom thing of his thin but muscular body? What would Tom's body be like, for they had never seen each other that way, naked and exposed? Maybe Tom would not want to be seen like that anyway. But what if they were to make love? Surely their love would overcome any imperfection they might have. How does one make love in situations like this? Questions, questions, doubts running through his head. These were broken suddenly by his mother's voice calling from the kitchen.

'It's nearly eleven o'clock. Don't you think you should be getting on the move?'

He lurched himself back into reality. God, he didn't want to be late. He felt his forehead. It felt hot and full of perspiration. He hurriedly washed his face in cold water and cleaned his teeth. Hurriedly he returned to his bedroom to look at himself in the long mirror. He brushed his hair down smooth and ran his fingers through his newly grown beard. It had done well in the short time he had been home. He wondered what Tom would think of it? He hurried downstairs, kissed his mother, and dashed out the front door and through the garden gate. Taking a deep breath, he headed off in the direction of the railway station. There was no doubt about it, he was feeling so much better now that he had something in his life to think of other than the horrors of war ingrained in his head.

His pace was brisk, and he hardly felt out of breath. Must be the swimming, he thought. As he approached the station, he suddenly began to feel nervous. He could see the time on the station clock. It was eleven forty five. The platform was almost empty apart from a young man sitting on one of the wicker baskets that was destined for the luggage compartment. From where he stood he looked very much like Doug sitting there. He couldn't be sure, but it looked very much like him. As he went to approach the porter busying himself with parcels to ask if there was a train due in, he was aware that the young man on the basket was waving to him. The porter told him that the train going to London was due to be arriving soon. He thanked him and started to make his way down the platform to a smiling Doug. Yes, it was him.

'How nice to see you again,' Doug offered as a greeting.

They shook hands. For a moment there was complete silence between them as their eyes search each other's. Doug was smiling, and his eyes were alive.

'Are you catching the train as well?' Doug asked.

'No I'm not travelling. You are off to London today then?'

'Yes. I was hoping that you would be travelling too. That would have been nice,' Doug continued.

There was the sound of the train in the distance and Doug looked up the track, then his gaze returned to Bryan again. For a moment neither of them spoke or made a move as their eyes remained in contact.

'I wish I had met up with you earlier. It's only the loneliness of the village that makes me want to get away from it all and find a new life.'

The train was drawing nearer now as they hurriedly tried to search each other for reactions.

'I think we could have become good friends. Maybe we can meet up again when I come home next time, or if it doesn't work out for me in London.'

'That would be nice,' Bryan managed to blurt out.

'Yes, wouldn't it,' Doug replied. ' I think you know what I mean.'

'Pardon. What are you saying?'

'I'm making a bloody mess of this conversation,' Doug said, looking away for a moment as the train rounded the bend and was drawing close to the other end of the platform. 'Look, can you phone me sometime?'

Doug hurriedly pulled out a letter from his jacket pocket and opened it.

'Have you got a pencil or something?' Doug asked.

'No. I don't think I have.'

He watched as Doug tore the address off of the letter and handed it to him.

'You can phone me there at that number.'

The train was now almost drawing close to them. Doug picked up his leather case as the trains smoke enveloped them both as they stood there. Doug stood aside as one of the doors opened, then turning sharply he threw the case inside the now empty carriage. He went to climb inside, but suddenly turned back onto the platform. He anxiously and nervously looked around them, and with one quick and desperate move, threw his arms around Bryan and drew their bodies together. It was only a quick hug, but enough to secure the friendship before they parted.

'Call me please,' Doug said as he leaned out of the carriage window.

Bryan was in a state of shock for a moment. He looked at Doug and smiled a nervous smile.

'I promise.'

The guard's whistle sounded and the train started to draw away. Bryan reached out his hand to Doug and their hands touched just for a second as the train moved off. They waved through the smoke from the engine. Then he was gone. He felt quite numb standing there for a moment. Then his thoughts hurriedly returned to the reason for being there on the platform in the first place. He looked up along the platform, which was vacant except for the porter who was dragging mailbags along the platform. There was no sign of Tom. He panicked for a moment. Maybe he had missed the train. Maybe he would be on the next. His head was still full of the reactions to Doug's departure. He stared to try and catch the porter before he disappeared out of sight. As he passed the ticket office, he saw a lonely figure standing there looking out into the car park. It was Tom.

'Tom,' he cried out.

'Bryan,' Tom said, turning to greet him. 'I couldn't see you anywhere.'

'How are you?'

'Fine I think.'

They stood there looking each other over with searching eyes. Tom extended his hand out and they shook hands in a formal manner. There was no hint of more than a friendly handshake between them, unlike the reactions of Doug.

'I was looking for your car,' Tom said.

'I'm afraid I haven't one. We walk everywhere down here. I'll help you carry your case.'

'No I'm fine. Need the muscle building exercise, Tom laughingly said. 'You've lost weight too I see. I like your beard. How long have you had that?' he said, reaching out to touch it.

'Oh. I grew it out of boredom. Glad you like it,' he said, sensing the tenderness of Tom's touch, or was that just wishful thinking?

'It's good of you to invite me down to stay a while. I needed to get away from everything back home, what with questions, and people staring at me,' Tom said, as they began to walk out of the station yard. 'How have you been?'

'I have found it hard to get myself out into the world again. To tell you the truth, I'm shit scared of meeting people.'

'Me too,' Tom said.

They walked in silence for a while. He watched Tom's expressions as he turned and glanced at him now and again. Tom smiled each time he caught him looking in his direction. Tom looked so different somehow. His features had changed, and he was even more handsome than he could have imagined. At other times he had only seen Tom in a raw state, with muddy features and wearing a helmet most of the time. He had seen him without his clothes on that day they found the tin bath at the farmhouse, but even then as there were so many others around at the time, it was not the time to stare. But what he did see of Tom was ingrained in his memory. How beautiful that slim body had been he recalled, as Tom had stood there waiting his turn to bathe. He remembered how he felt on seeing the sun gleaming across Tom's wet back, and the smile he had on his face as he had caught him looking at him. That was the moment he realised that he had feelings for Tom, and about the only time he had felt his groin stir during those terrible days of fighting the Germans.

'You are deep in thought,' Tom suddenly said. 'Where were you?'

Bryan blushed at the question, but only shook his head.

'I don't mind not talking,' Tom said.' I just want to let my head clear a bit. If I do want to talk I want to talk about anything other than the war. I just want to be left alone, but with someone I have a deep understanding with.'

Bryan looked at Tom as he said these words. For a moment they just looked at each other. Then, to his surprise, Tom attempted to put his arm around his shoulder pulling them closer together. Bryan tried to do the same back, but his arm seemed to loose control and he ended up just bumping into Tom. They smiled at each other. This was a break through, Bryan thought. He suddenly felt nervous, yet excited. He began thinking as to how his mother would react to Tom. He hoped she liked him.

'We're nearly there,' he said, looking up the lane and pointing towards the cottage.

'So peaceful,' Tom said.

'I think you'll like it here. We have a river running along the back of our gardens. Do you swim?'

'A bit,' Tom smiled. 'Do you swim a lot in it then?'

'Have done since I was a teenager. I used to swim with my sisters a lot.'

'Oh. You have sisters then?'

'Yes. I thought I'd told you that.'

'No. Are they living in the cottage?'

Bryan, for a moment could sense an interest in his sisters coming from Tom.

'They left home long ago. The only person in the cottage now is my mum.'

Tom's face seemed to light up having heard this.

'Here we are then. My home,' Bryan said, as they arrived at the front gate of the cottage.

'This looks homely' Tom said.

'Come on in and meet my mum.'

Bryan pushed the front door open. It was never really shut until bedtime. There was a smell of cooking in the air.

'Leave your case there and come into the kitchen. We almost live in there. Hello mum, I'm back. This is Tom. Tom my mum.'

Tom offered his hand out to Bryan's mum. She eyed him up and down for a moment and smiled as she shook hands with him.

'Heard a lot about you young man. You are very welcome.'

'Well thank you. It's nice to have a welcome like that,' Tom said, looking around the kitchen. 'Nice little cottage you have here,' he said, trying to make light conversation.

'I'll make you a cup of tea. I expect you are thirsty after that long journey?'

'That would be nice,' Tom said.

Bryan, sensing the slight awkwardness of the first introduction of Tom to his mother suggested that he took Tom out into the garden until tea was made.

'Give us a call mum when teas ready. I'll just show Tom the garden.'

Tom looked relieved and followed him out through the back door.

'The toilet is there,' Bryan said, pointing to the paint weary wooden door at the end of the cottage.

'I could use that now if I may,' Tom said. I didn't want to ask your mum.'

Bryan watched Tom enter and close the door. He waited down the garden under the apple tree. He could feel his mother watching their every move. He wondered if she was beginning to think he was more than a friend to him, but then his mother wouldn't know about things like that. Tom joined him and they started to walk down the path leading to the meadow. They talked about anything and yet nothing as they were searching for signs from each other that they wanted contact.

Bryan pointed to the spot where he and his sisters and mother used to picnic at.

'Happy memories I bet,' Tom said.

'Yes. God I wish I could have stayed back in those days. They were secure days.'

'Did you have a girlfriend back then?' Tom asked.

Bryan hesitated with his reply. He was being tested.

'No. Not really.'

The answer was passed over quickly by Tom. There was an awkward silence for a moment.

'Have you ever loved anyone?' Bryan asked, searching Tom's face for the answer.

'Yes. But I don't think they knew it at the time.'

There was silence again. They walked slowly through the tall grass, both tearing shoots from the sheaths and sucking the sweet tasting juice from the stems. They were both deep in thought as they reached the river. They stood there on the bank mesmerised by the flowing water.

'We used to swim down stream to our favourite tree trunk,' Bryan said.

Tom removed the grass shoot from his mouth and tossed it into the water. They both watched it flow down stream.

'Hope we can get a swim in this week,' Bryan said. 'It's great in the early evening as the sun goes down. The waters quite warm after a day's sun on it.'

'Sounds good. But I don't have a costume.'

'We didn't bother with them. I don't think my mum knew we skinny-dipped like that. We used to dip our costumes in the water to get them wet before we went home. I don't think she would have let us go if she knew,' Bryan laughed.

The subject got passed over quickly. Bryan thought that this had made Tom embarrassed. They turned around and headed back to the cottage. Bryan wanted Tom to show some sign of wanting to touch or hold him like he had in the trench that time. Although he was feeling a pain in the pit of his stomach, he resisted the gnawing temptation to embrace him. They walked in silence. His mother was waiting for their return. She stood looking out of the kitchen window at them.

'Where have you been? Your tea will be getting cold in the pot if you don't drink it soon.'

'Sorry mum. Can we have it in the garden?'

The tray was placed on the wooden bench table by mum. She just placed it down but never poured.

'I'm off to the shops, so if you are wandering off again, tea will be at five o'clock,' she said.' Show Tom his room wont you.'

They watched her go back into the cottage before Bryan started to pour the tea.

'Your mum's nice and homely,' Tom said. 'Do you mind if I take my shoes off?'

'Go ahead. Do you take sugar?'

'One lump please.'

Bryan watched as Tom removed his boots and massaged his right foot. He could see he was feeling some pain. Tea being poured, they sat back on opposite sides of the table. Tom stretched out and rested his feet at the side of were Bryan sat. He had no idea what prompted him to do it, but he gave in to the temptation to take hold of Tom's troubled foot and started to gently massage it for him. Although it was a simple contact, the feeling that ran through his body made him feel good. He looked at Tom for a reaction. Tom smiled as he sat back with a satisfied look on his face.

'That feels good,' Tom said.

You have no idea how good that feels for me too, Bryan was thinking. How he wanted to take this first intimate contact further. The most adventurous he got was to run his hand around Tom's ankle. But at least he didn't get a rejection. Without realising it, their eyes made contact every few seconds. There was chemistry running between them, and this was exciting for Bryan, and gave him hope that this was the start of something greater than just being friends. It was strange but they hardly mentioned the war. It was as if they wanted to block the horrors out of their minds.

'I'll show you your room while mums out. She has been worried all week that you might not like it. It hasn't been used for a few years now.' He wanted to say something like '*I wish you could sleep with me in my room*' but he didn't dare to suggest that. Tom carried his case upstairs into his bedroom. He placed it down on the bed and went to look out of the window at the view. Bryan joined him.

'What a nice place to live,' Tom said

They both leaned side by side on the window ledge to take in the view that Bryan had too often taken for granted.

'It's not so far to the river then. It seemed further than that when we walked it earlier,' Tom said.

Bryan nodded. He could feel their shoulders touching, and it felt so good. His stomach gave a churning noise. They laughed together.

'It's so good to be away from home and all the questions. But I've said that before. What I really meant to say was that I'm glad to have found you again. Shit, I thought you were dead.'

They remained silent again as they stared out of the window with shoulders touching, neither quite knowing what was going on inside then. Bryan desperately wanted to make the first move to have physical contact with Tom. Was it too soon to make his move? Would he be rejected? They remained silent for a while. Then suddenly Tom moved and turned towards the bed to open his case. Bryan felt the strength go from his legs suddenly and he remained leaning on the window ledge for support. He was sure that Tom was not going to respond to any of his moves. Oh God.

'I've brought you something, and something for your mother,' Tom suddenly said.

Bryan turned his head around to look back as he heard the noise of the case being clipped open.

'Stay there, and keep your eyes closed. Don't look,' Tom said, rustling through his case.

Bryan waited. He could hear Tom coming across the room behind him. He wanted to turn and look.

'There you are. Hope you like it,' Tom said, as he leaned once again on the window ledge with him. 'You can open your eyes now you daft sod.'

Bryan took hold of the small parcel wrapped in brown paper. He turned around and placed his back against the window frame. He looked at Tom's expression as he began to unwrap the parcel.

'What have we got here, Bryan said, as he untied the string with his hands shaking. Not with excitement as much, but frustration in not being able to bring himself to make the first move. Bryan watched him struggle with undoing the knots in the string. They laughed a nervous laugh together.

'Here. Let me help,' Tom said.

Bryan held the quite small parcel in his hands as Tom tried to untie the knot.

'There you are,' Tom said, as the knot finally broke free, and he left Bryan to undo the rest.

'Soap,' Bryan suddenly cried out. French bloody soap. Where the hell did you get that from?'

'You remembered then. You remembered the day we all took that bath outside that farmhouse?'

'Could I ever forget,' Bryan replied. 'Is this the same soap we all had to share?'

'Yes. I managed to get hold of some for you. I thought you would like some to remind you. Stupid really I suppose. Could have bought you a book to read.'

'No really. This is nice. I loved the smell of French soap,' he said, as he brought the four bars of soap under his nose to smell the fragrance. It brought back memories of that special day.

Tom leaned forward to smell the soap as well. Their faces came close together, and as if it had been designed this way especially for the opportunity, Bryan placed a gentle kiss on Tom's cheek. It was only a brief encounter, but it was an amazing intimate moment. They looked into each other's eyes and searched for those magical signs that could say more than words. Bryan's eyes were alive and full of expectation. Tom's eyes were alive, but there was something that seemed to question the act.

Bryan blushed, looked down and continued back to smell the soap. He had judged Tom wrongly. He felt embarrassed and at a loss as to what to do next.

'I'm sorry,' Bryan said, looking up again.

Tom just smiled, then turned away to continue to unpack his case.

Bryan left the room not quite knowing how he could explain to Tom his feelings for him. He went into his own bedroom that was across the narrow landing and sat down on his bed. His head was full of thoughts. He smelt the soap again, and it rushed the scene into his head of them taking a bath outside the farmhouse in France. He could remember the feelings that ran through his body as he watched Tom soaping himself in that tin bath in the farmyard. How he had wanted to put his arms around him, as he stood there afterwards, naked, trying to dry himself with his own army shirt. The sight of his strong athletic back and pert buttocks, plus his coyness in front of the other troops in trying to hide his modesty, made him want to comfort him there and then.

His thoughts were interrupted as he heard a tap on his door. He hurriedly put down his present of soap on the dressing table, then collected himself.

'Come in,' he called out.

Tom put his head around the door and smiled at him again. He was holding another parcel in his hand as he stood there looking a little lost in the world.

'I'm sorry,' Bryan eventually managed to say. 'I just felt like saying - *thank you*- for my present.'

'You daft bugger. Look, can I give this to your mum?'

'Yes. Just go on down into the kitchen, she'll be there doing something. She'll love it.'

He sat there listening to the sound of Tom's footsteps going down the stairs. He could hear a conversation going on between the two of them and the odd word drifted upstairs clearly for him to hear. His mother had taken a liking to Tom by the way she gave out the odd laugh or two. This was a sure sign that she approved of him, for it was rare that his mother laughed like that so openly.

That evening as they sat around the kitchen table eating and drinking, he watched Tom's every move. The more he watched, the more he just wanted to be closer to him to hold him. Tom and his mother had almost finished eating, but he was struggling to eat at all.

'Come on Bryan, you haven't hardly eaten a thing. Are you not feeling well?'

'I'm fine thanks. Just not as hungry as you I guess,' he said, picking at his food with his fork again.

The plates were cleared away and mother started washing up. Tom picked up a tea towel and began wiping up at her side. Bryan sat there watching the two of them, laughing at the way Tom tried to guess which cupboard or draw each item went in. He was such a nice bloke. Once the two of them had finished the washing up, his mother said she was ready for an early night, and would leave the two of them to talk. She kissed Bryan on his cheek and ran her hands across his back as she began to make her move upstairs. As she passed where Tom was sitting, she placed a gentle kiss on the top of his head in passing. He looked up and smiled at her.

'Goodnight. Don't forget to lock up. See you in the morning. Sleep tight,' she said. Then she was gone. For a while the two sat there in silence. Bryan reached forward and opened the doors of the range to let the firelight enter the room. It was warm and cosy all of a sudden. He watched as the firelight flickered across Tom. Oh God he couldn't carry on like this. If only Tom would give him some sign that he wanted to return the love he had for him then maybe the pain in his body would be relieved. Tom answered the odd question about where he lived and his family, but they were struggling for conversation. It was nearly ten o'clock when Bryan suggested that it was time for bed. They shut the doors of the range, locked up, and headed upstairs together. As Tom went to open his bedroom door, Bryan wanted to kiss him or hold him for a moment, but he knew that was not the right timing. Tom hesitated, turned as if to make contact and just for a second Bryan's hopes were raised, but Tom turned away again.

'Goodnight,' Tom said quietly.

'Goodnight,' Bryan replied.

Their doors closed, and they were in their own worlds again.

Bryan sat on the edge of his bed with head in his hands, frustrated and dejected. He wondered how he could test out Tom's sexuality. He never talked much about his feelings for others, but there were signs that he approved of their moments of physical contact, yet he never made the moves that where signs that he wanted to take things further. He heard Tom's door open and the sound of his footsteps along the landing. The bathroom door opened and closed gently. Maybe he could time it right and make his own move towards the bathroom so as he could have a chance of making contact again with him one more time before they slept. He stood listening at his door with his towel over his bare shoulder. He heard the bathroom door open, and he turned the handle of his door to open it at the same time. The landing was in darkness, but he could make out Tom turning to go back to his room. For a moment they just stood still not wanting to disturb Bryan's mother. His eyes quickly ran over Tom's bare chest. It was the first time he had seen him naked from the waist up since that time in France. He looked so lean yet well toned with a hairless chest. He could just make out the fine line of dark hair just appearing under his naval so tantalisingly tempting. They smiled at each other in the dimness of the night. Not a word was spoken. Tom opened the bathroom door again for him, and the sudden shaft of moonlight sculptured Tom's body with light and shadow as he stood there holding the door open. He squeezed past Tom, and just for a second their bodies came into contact. They both hesitated in the doorway.

Oh how he wanted to embrace Tom there and then.

'Goodnight,' Tom whispered.

Words would not come out for him to reply so he just reached out and touched Tom's bare shoulder with a pat. To his delight Tom responded by running his hand across his shoulder in return. It was the first intimate moment they had had since those moments in the trenches. He felt his legs wobble. How he wished Tom would enter the bathroom with him, but no. The door closed behind him, and once again an opportunity had passed.

CHAPTER 6

Doug had arrived in London and walked what seemed miles to find his lodgings. He found Goode Street, and now all he had to do was to find number one five two. Just his luck he thought, it had to be at he other end of the street. He looked up at the old Victorian buildings. They were dirty and uninviting he thought. He rang the bell and leaned back against the iron railings waiting for the door to be opened. There was no reply, so he rang again. The door suddenly opened and the stern face of an elderly woman appeared.

'Yes?' she asked, looking first at him then up and down the street.

'I'm Doug Vine. I think I have a room waiting for me here.'

The woman studied him from top to toe. Then she suddenly stood aside and ushered him inside. Once inside the hall, Doug placed his case down on the rather worn hall rug. He went to extend his hand out to her, but by the looks of her, she was not the type to be that welcoming. He looked around him. The hall was dark and the only lighting he could see was two gas wall lights. It was not a welcoming hallway. The accommodation had been arranged by his friend the printer he was going to work for. Not a good start he thought.

'I'll show you your room,' the woman said.

As she climbed the stairs in front of him, he could hear her muttering to herself. They reached the landing, and there was a little more light coming in through a window at the far end. The net curtains looked as if they had been hanging there for many a year without attention.

'This is your room,' she said, opening a door and walking inside to stand with her arms folded across her rather full bosoms. Her face had not showed any signs of being friendly. 'No visitors, and you have to be indoors by ten o'clock else you will have to find somewhere else to stay.'

He looked around the room that was to be his home. It had not been decorated for years. There was a small window, which did not let in very much daylight. At the side of the single bed stood a well-used chair. On the other side of the bed was a chest of draws, and on top rested a wash bowl and jug. Above the bed was a gas lamp, and apart from a wardrobe, that was the extent of his comforts.

'I don't know your name,' Doug suddenly said, his words just croaked out from his dry throat.

'Mr's Dobson,' she replied. Bathroom's up there along the landing. Baths are extra, and no visitors.' Doug smiled inwardly at her remark as he twisted it around in his mind as meaning - *no visitors in the bathroom.* As she made her way out of his dingy room, he closed the door behind her, then leaned his back against it. This was not what he had expected. How he wished he was at home again in his own room. His thoughts then were for his brief meeting with Bryan on the platform, and that brief kiss. There had been something about Bryan that made his inside screw up. Why had he not met up with him before he had made up his mind to come down to London?

He unpacked his clothes from his case and hung them up in the wardrobe on the three hangers provided. He placed his shirts and jumpers in the chest of draws. The wash bowl and jug rattled as he closed the ill-fitting draws. This was to be his home for his stay in London. His depression did not diminish as he lay down on the bed. The springs under the hard mattress played a dismal tune with his every movement. It was just as well that he was not allowed visitors, he thought to himself.

Sleep did not come easy that night. He was hungry and tired from his journey, yet sleep did not come until around three in the morning. The knock on his door, and the call of *'breakfast'* was almost a welcome awakening. He would have liked to have taken a bath if he had not been rationed to two a week. Pulling on his trousers he made his way into the bathroom to fill his water jug. As the water started to fill, he glanced at the enamel bath with its stained watermarks. It was far from inviting. Back in his room he hurriedly stripped himself naked and ran a wet flannel over his body. At least this freshened him up a little ready for the working day. Breakfast was porridge, a mug of tea, and a kipper on a cold plate. He could feel the eyes of Mrs Dobson watching his every move. She was a woman of few words, so when it came to asking her directions to the printer's shop he was due to start at he had to listen hard, for she was not about to repeat her directions again for him.

Somehow he felt much better for leaving the house. The air was fresh and the streets damp with an early morning mist that seemed to hang around the soot grime grey houses. He tried to remember the directions he was given. London was a world away from his own little village. He looked up at a clock that stood out from one of the buildings. He was running late. By the time he reached the doors of the print shop, he was almost out of breath from having had to run the last few hundred yards to make up time. As he opened the door and entered, the smell of printing inks and spirits reached his nostrils and entered his lungs like a sharp knife. The noise of the print presses thundered in his head, and for a moment he felt like turning away and running from his future. It was having sight of his friend Dick approaching him that stopped him in his tracks.

'Well you made it then,' Dick said, standing there wiping his ink splattered hands with a cloth.

'Just,' Doug shouted out.

'Come into the office,' Dick said, walking through the masses of paper piles and tins of inks lying around the floor making it difficult to follow. As the door of the tiny office closed, it was a relief to have the noise of the print shops muffled.

'Take a seat,' Dick said, pointing to a wooden box the other side of the desk that was piled with papers and files and bundles of printed matter.

'As you will see, I need help. How are you?' Dick asked.

Doug sat down and looked around the cluttered office. He smiled. Dick did need help. He had changed as well. He looked older than the last time they had met. Somehow he looked less appealing. There had been a time when they had been close back home. They were both in their teens when they discovered gay sex together. It had been fun at first, but then it began to get serious. At first they wrestled and romped in the fields that surrounded the village. It had been fun, but they knew they were exploring each other's bodies at the same time.

Then came the day when it was taken further than just a romp in the grass. They had wrestled for ages, laughing as they pinned each other down. Dick had been the first to make that fatal move that changed their lives and confirmed their sexuality. He had been wanting Dick to attempt to grope between his thighs and hold his erection. Their wrestling ended immediately and they lay there on their sides staring into each other's eyes searching for reactions. Before long they had found themselves naked under the sun and exploring each other's bodies in an awkward fashion at first. Then as the days passed they had ventured further until the guilt overcame their naivety of what they were getting into.

'Coffee?' Dick asked, bringing him back to the real world again.

'Thanks. Coffee would be fine.'

He watched Dick as he dashed out of the office to check one of the machines. The noise of the printing machines thumped through his head. As he stood up to close the door, he could see Dick down the far end of the workshop now, boiling up a kettle on a gas ring. Yes, Dick had got much older. Maybe he had made a mistake in taking up the offer of working for him. Maybe it had not been the work that had made his mind up at the time, but the thought that they might return to those teen years again. Maybe he had made a terrible mistake in coming to London.

CHAPTER 7

He had not slept hardly at all on the first night Tom had slept over in the cottage. For most of the night Bryan had sat up in his bed with his pillow in his arms and his head buried deep into it for comfort. There was a deep pain raging through his body as he desperately yearned to be with Tom.

He was sure that he had seen every hour pass him through the night, and when he heard that knock on his door and the sound of the handle being turned, he had hoped that it was Tom.

'It's a lovely morning. You should both be up and out in the fresh air.'

It was his mother with early morning tea. His heart sank, and he hid his head under the bedclothes to shield his eyes from the sunlight as his mother opened the curtains to let the morning in.

'Morning mum.'

'Good morning my dear.'

'Is Tom up?'

'I've brought his tea up with me. Maybe you might like to take it into him for me.'

His head cleared instantly. It was the thought of having a reason to enter Tom's room that made him sit up quickly in his bed. There on the bedside cabinet were two mugs of tea. He ran his fingers through his hair as he hurried out of bed. Pulling on his dressing gown, he checked himself out in the mirror. He wished he had had a better night's sleep. His knock on the door was answered.

'Come in.'

Tom was lying with his hands behind his head on the pillow with the bedclothes covering his nakedness from just above his waist. The two of them exchanged looks. Oh, how inviting Tom looked lying there having just woken up with that dreamy look about him.

'I've brought you your tea. Do you mind if I join you?'

Tom patted the bed and smiled.

If only he could be less reserved, Bryan thought, as he passed Tom his tea. He could have taken it that Tom wanted him to join him in bed by the way he had patted the bed at the side of him. But he dare not assume anything from this gesture, so he sat down on the edge of the bed instead.

'Did you sleep well?' Bryan asked.

'I never sleep well on the first night in a strange bed,' Tom replied. 'How about you?'

'Restless night.'

They sipped at their tea in silence for a while.

'I should have given you a book to read or something, ' Bryan said, breaking the silence.

'I needed something. I hate just lying there trying not to think of the war.'

'If you have another night like that, you should knock on my door,' Bryan said, wishing he hadn't.

Tom smiled over the top of his mug of tea at the offer and reached out to take hold of Bryan's hand.

'Thanks for inviting me down here for a break, I need someone to share with. It's been hell dealing with memories on my own.'

Bryan took hold of Tom's hand. It felt soft and warm in his palm. They remained like that for a while before talking again. Was this a sign that Tom wanted to have physical contact with him? The feel of Tom's warm hand in his, flooded his whole body with emotional charges. How he wanted to be at his side in bed just to hold him. He was sure that Tom would want to be more intimate than just holding his hand. But at least this was a good sign, and he should not read too much into this first encounter.

'Would you like a bath this morning?' Bryan asked.

'Could I?'

'Sure. I'll run it for you in a moment.'

They finished their tea, and Bryan felt that he should remain calm and controlled with his actions. But the more he saw of Tom, the more he wanted to have him. He caught Tom looking at him as he stared at the bare chest lying there in bed. How he wished to reach out and make that first move. Being aware that he had been caught staring, he moved off of the bed. His dressing gown parted a little as he slithered himself off the bed. He caught Tom watching his every move. They smiled at each other, and Bryan was sure now that Tom was warming to the relationship.

'I'll run the bath for you.'

'Thanks.'

He left the bedroom and hurried down stairs with the two empty mugs. His mother was in the kitchen as usual. He placed the mugs down by the sink, then placed his arms around her rounded waist. Her head turned to receive his kiss on her cheek.

'Did you sleep well mum?'

'Not bad.'

'I'm going to run a bath for Tom.'

'Don't use all the hot water. I'll have to stoke the boiler up again.'

'Don't worry. I'll probably jump in his water after him to save you doing that.'

'Good-heavens. You can't do that.'

'Mum, I'm used to sharing a bath with more than Tom.'

His mother just shook her head as she continued washing up. She smiled to herself as she remembered the times she used to have to share the tin bath in front of the kitchen range with her sisters and brothers. But the thought of sharing a bath with strangers or friends, oh no.

The bath was three quarter full when Tom appeared from his bedroom with a bath towel wrapped around his waist. The two of them stood together at the side of the bath for a moment. Bryan suddenly felt that Tom was waiting for him to exit the room, and he began to feel uncomfortable.

But to his surprise and delight, Tom removed his towel and started to climb into the bath.

He watched as Tom lowered himself slowly into the hot water.

'This is just what I needed. It's ages since I had a hot bath like this,' Tom said. 'Remember the bath we had outside that farmhouse?'

Bryan smiled. If only Tom knew how well he had remembered that day, and the feelings that had ran through his body as he had watched on. But now, with the scene being much more intimate, he could hardly keep his eyes off of Tom. He had a gorgeous lithe body, and he was well endowed, so much so that he had to resist staring as Tom lay there with the water movements making the moment fell so sensuous.

'Leave the water in the bath when you've finished. I'll jump in it as that's the last of the hot water for the morning.'

'Oh, I'm sorry. You should have said. I'll hurry up then before it gets cold.'

'Just give me a shout when you are getting out.'

Back in his bedroom he could hear the water splashing around in the bath. Oh how he wished he could be bold enough to join Tom and share the bath together. He sat there in his dressing gown waiting for Tom to call out. His mind was playing games with him. Just as he was fantasying about sharing the bath, there was a knock on his door. Thinking that it was his mother about to enter he quickly crossed his legs to cover his fast growing erection. But to his horror he heard Tom call out that the bathroom was free. Then there was the sound of Tom's bedroom door closing. He felt deflated and emotionally drained for his mind had played the role of the two of them engaging in some form of contact in the bathroom, but this was not to be. He lowered himself into the now tepid bath water and hurriedly soaped himself down. How he wished Tom to come into the bathroom now. Was he asking too much of this friendship? Maybe Tom was far from wanting him.

All he knew was, he almost cried aloud with wanting Tom. He knew he couldn't go on much longer without making the first move. What if Tom was to reject his advances? God, he would just die. As he stood there drying himself down with his towel, he thought he heard a door open and close down the landing. His heart started to beat faster with anticipation. He held his breath so as to hear any movement coming his way. How he longed for the door to open. He waited, then slowly went over to the door, turned the door handle, and looked through the narrowest of openings in hope. The landing was clear. Tom must have gone down stairs. He hurriedly dried himself and ventured out onto the landing. There were voices coming from downstairs. He thumped his hand against the door frame in frustration as he entered his room to get dressed. When he got himself downstairs and entered the kitchen, Tom was sitting at the table talking to his mother. He turned his head and greeted him with a smile.

'Hope the bath water was not too cold for you. I hurried as much as I could.'

Bryan walked around the table and passed the back of Tom's chair. He couldn't resist running his hand across Tom's back. Tom looked up and smiled again.

'You two should get some fresh-air today. You look quite pale to me Bryan,' his mother said.

'I'm fine mum. But I think you are right. Shall we walk along the river today Tom?'

'Fine by me,' Tom replied.

'Well sit down and eat your breakfast first,' his mother said, placing the plates down in front of them. 'You both need to get some meat on your ribs,' she said, looking at them both in turn.

Breakfast over, the two of them stood side by side at the sink washing up. For a while they fooled around giving nudges of their bodies trying to unbalance each other like schoolboys do. Then some soap bubbles splashed up onto Bryan's face. Tom laughed and gently wiped the soap away with the tea towel. Then, to Bryan's surprise, Tom placed a gentle kiss on his cheek, having looked quickly around the kitchen to see if Bryan's mother was looking. Bryan froze on the spot. Their playing stopped, and there was a sudden urge for Bryan to return the gesture. Their eyes searched each other's. There was chemistry flowing between them, Bryan was sure of that now. The mood was broken as mother presented them with the breadboard for washing up.

CHAPTER 8

They could feel mother's eyes watching them as they headed down the garden path together and walk through the garden and into the meadow beyond. The day was sunny and hot as they walked in silence. The river was running high and the rushing sounds of the water seemed to pad out their silence. They had just started to walk along the tow-path when Tom turned and offered his hand out to Bryan to take hold of. It was such a simple gesture, yet in his haste to take hold, Bryan fumbled his grip. They stopped for a moment and faced each other.

'Did you mind what I did back there in the kitchen?' Tom suddenly asked.

'Not at all,' Bryan replied, his voice wobbled an octave higher than normal.

There was silence again between them as they continued walking. What was it that made him so insecure and nervous about making his first move? Bryan was thinking. He was sure that Tom was inviting him to go further with their relationship.

'I have to say the river does look inviting,' Tom suddenly said. 'Did you really swim without costumes even with your sisters?'

'Yes. We grew up like that together.'

'What about friends?'

'Not really. The blokes that were around when I was sixteen weren't into that sort of thing. It was all football and girls. I did have a friend called Ian who did come swimming with me one summer, but he got all stupid about it.'

Tom gave a little laugh.

'He spoiled it. Soon he and his other mates came down and fucked around. It wasn't quite the same after that. But, I went swimming with Tina, my sister, when she came down to see me.'

'Not sure that I could do that,' Tom said, with a frown on his face.

'Why is that?' Bryan asked, searching for a reason.

'I just wouldn't feel comfortable.'

'What if was your sister?'

Tom just shrugged his shoulders, and continued walking.

'Would you be uncomfortable swimming with me then?' Bryan asked, searching for a clue as to Tom's preferences or choice in company. Did that mean he didn't like women so much, and had a preference for men? Oh, how he wished this was true.

They walked along the tow-path and reached the willow tree once more. Tom knelt down and felt the temperature of the water. He stayed there swishing his hand around in the water for a while.

'I think I might like to take a dip this evening with you,' Tom suddenly said.

'That could be fun,' Bryan said, wishing that he had rephrased that statement.

They walked back towards the cottage again. It was when they reached the meadow with its deep grass that Tom stopped for a moment and looked around him.

'What a beautiful place. Is this where you used to have your picnics?

Bryan nodded and began to sit down on the grass. He watched Tom standing there in the sunlight. He was a fine looking man. If only he was to respond to my feelings, he thought. But then, how could he because he hadn't made the first approach. God, if only he could bring himself to pluck- up courage and maybe try to kiss him back. Tom looked down at him, and then he made a move to join him in the long grass. He pulled another blade of grass and tried to make whistling sounds through holding the grass between his thumbs and blowing. He laughed at his failed attempts.

'I used to be able to do that,' he said.'

They both laughed nervously as their shoulders nudged against each other. Tom threw the reed of grass away and started to tug off his shirt over his head. Bryan watched the smooth taunt flesh of Tom's body slowly appear. Tom lay on his back with his hands behind his head and closed his eyes for a moment. Bryan's heart beat faster as he looked at what was a body so beautiful and inviting laying there at his side. He had to make his move now. His whole body trembled as he ventured to reach out and place his hand across Tom's taunt stomach muscles. Tom let out a slight murmur and his muscles gave a slight tightening action. Was this the sign of approval he had wanted to hear? Not a word was spoken as Bryan's hand gently ran over the taunt flesh, so warm and inviting. As his hand started to drift down to the top of Tom's trousers and then back again, he watched for reactions. There were none. Slowly he started to undo the first of the buttons, as there was no belt to worry or inhibit his actions. His hand ventured inside now, and he could feel the pubic hair against his fingertips. For a moment he stopped his searching. There was no sign of an erection that he had hoped to find. His fingers touched on the flaccid penis that lay between Tom's thighs. Bryan's eyes searched into Tom's. There was a sense of bewilderment on Tom's face as he lay there, still with hands behind his head. Then to Bryan's relief his hand felt the movement in the depths of Tom's trousers as an erection began to be felt. Still not a word was spoken. Bryan began to undo the remaining buttons and opened the fly wide apart. He watched as Tom's erection came to life. With a quick look at Tom's face again, he reached down to give pleasure to his lover. They both shuddered at the first touch. He had never held another man like this before. Tom moaned, yet never attempted to stop him in making love this way. The feeling was mind blowing for both lovers. Tom had still made no attempt to stop his seducer. Bryan quickened his pace of stroke and Tom raised his buttocks a little from the ground in response. The climax came far too soon for Bryan. He watched as the love juices suddenly, and without warning, erupted high onto Tom's stomach. The moment passed so quickly that Bryan began to feel a sense of guilt coming over him. He looked at Tom's face again. There was only a slight hint of a half smile for a second or two, but then it faded. Tom rolled over onto his side and away from Bryan a fraction. Not a word was spoken. Bryan had his own erection now to deal with.

Oh, how he wished Tom would do the same for him. Moments later, Tom looked over his shoulder a caught sight of Bryan's actions in the long grass some distance away. He guessed what he was doing. Quite sometime later the two walked almost separately back towards the cottage. Bryan so much wanted to throw his arms around Tom and caress and kiss him so as to make the world right again. Back in the cottage they were greeted with a cup of tea, which meant they had to converse with mum.

'Where did you go?' she asked.

She looked both of them in turn searching for one of them to answer her.

'Oh, just along the river,' Bryan told her.

'It was nice and sunny out there. But you would have been in the shade a lot,' mum continued. You both look a little flushed.'

'We sunbathed a little in the meadow,' Bryan said, hoping that this would settle the questioning.

'Ah, the sun has blessed you both.'

'Don't know about that,' Bryan replied.

Later that evening, when his mother had vacated the kitchen, Bryan suggested going for a swim after tea. Tom had been very silent through the afternoon. He looked thoughtful as he sat there reading a book.

'You go. I'd prefer to stay and read.

Bryan listened to see if he could hear his mother. He heard footsteps upstairs, which meant he had a few moments to say what he had to say to Tom.

'Are you upset with me?'

'No.

Then what's the matter?'

'Nothing.'

'You can't just say that. Did you not want me to do that to you?'

'I don't know. I really don't know. Sorry, but you go for your swim. I'll stay here.'

'I'm sorry, but when you gave me that kiss…I hoped that this meant… Bryan spluttered.'

Tom just looked at him, then returned to his book.

The evening was, or would have been, perfect for a swim. As Bryan removed his clothes and lowered himself down under the water, it flashed through his head that it might be the way out of his misery by staying under the surface. He surfaced immediately. What a foolish thought to have.

He swam upstream and caught hold of the willow tree when he reached it. He suddenly felt a little more secure as he dragged himself up onto the broken bough. He sat there wondering about his life and the pains he was going through in wrestling with his sexuality. How he wished he could be normal. Then he laughed to himself.

Normal... What did normal mean? He had been with mates in the army that were married. Jesus, most of them were far from normal in their relationships. They would have it away with any woman that was prepared to give herself to them. If that's normal, then he was glad that he was gay. He lay back on the tree trunk deep in thought. It was getting quite dark by the time he made his way back to the cottage. As he wandered through the meadow he could see the lights burning in the kitchen and upstairs room that Tom was sleeping in. As he entered the kitchen his mother turned away from the kitchen range where she had been cooking.

'Tom has gone to bed with his book. Poor lad seems unhappy about something.'

'Really. I'll go up and see him before I turn in,' Bryan said.

'I'm off to bed now,' his mother said, turning to kiss him as she made her way upstairs.

Somehow the cottage seemed silent, and he felt suddenly alone. He hung out his unused costume as usual. One day his mother would rumble him and about his skinny- dipping. Turning off the lights he began to make his way upstairs. As he passed Tom's room, the lights were out. He listened, but there were no sounds coming from within. Once again those sinking feelings ripped through his stomach as he yearned to be with Tom. Once in bed the feelings would not leave him. Tom was rejecting him he was sure, or was it that he was not sure about his sexuality like himself? He sat there in bed with his knees pulled up to his chin and his arms wrapped around them for comfort.

Had he been too clumsy in his first attempt to make love to Tom? Tom had not rejected him, yet he had not returned his love. He still had the feeling of Tom's erect cock in his hand, so firm and smooth to hold. His body trembled with tension. What was he to do to gain Tom's love in return? He tried masturbating himself for comfort, but even that was a failure, so he gave up on himself. Sleep did not come easy that night. He was pleased, yet annoyed, in seeing the sunrise lighting up his room for was this the beginning of another day's torment, or was it to be the start of day filled with love? As he slipped into his robe and made his way along the landing to the bathroom, Tom's door was still closed. But then it was only early morning yet. As he washed and cleaned his teeth his mind was busy again. Standing there over the basin, he made his mind up to confront Tom about his act yesterday, because he could not continue to live with these pangs of desire for the love of Tom. With his heart beating so fast that he felt he was going to faint, he tapped on Tom's door and began to enter. He could hear Tom breathing as if still asleep. Maybe he should leave him like that and leave the room, but he looked so beautiful lying there with the top half of his body exposed above the bedclothes. His bed was in a mess. It looked as if he had had a disturbed night as well. Just as he was about to turn and leave, Tom stirred in his sleep. His eyes opened, he looked at Bryan, then turned his head sideways on his pillow away from him for a moment. The he looked back at Bryan again. This time his eyes showed a brightness that said welcome.

'Hello. Did you have a good night, or did you have a rough night like me?' Tom said, reaching out a hand to be held.

'I had a bad night too,' Bryan said, taking hold of Tom's hand.

Tom drew Bryan towards him, and Bryan sat on the edge of the bed. Their eyes searched each other's for signs they were both desperate to see.

'I'm sorry for yesterday,' Bryan said.

'Don't be. It was my fault.'

'Why do you say that?'

'Well I think I made the first move with that kiss.'

'Didn't you mean it then?'

'Yes of cause I did,' Tom said.

'Then why did you let me...'

'I don't know. I really don't know,' Tom said, lying on his back again and searching the ceiling for answers to the question. There was a long silence. Then he suddenly felt Bryan's hand searching under the bedclothes and come to rest across his chest. A finger teased his nipple and it hardened instantly to the touch. His mind suddenly became confused, and his erection returned. His hand slithered down under the bedclothes and he took hold of it. There was a suggestion of moist love juice beginning to form on its bulbous head. God, what was going on? He was unable to help himself. He was entering into a scene that he was not used to, yet he was beginning to enjoy the sensation. Suddenly he could feel Bryan's hand touching his and removing it away from his now rock hard penis. He gave no resistance to the move. The two remained silent as Bryan worked his hand in slow rhythmic strokes up and down Toms' erect shaft. He parted his legs to allow Bryan the freedom to perform the act.

The act didn't last long though, and they both tried to smother the eruption with their hands so as not to soil the sheets. There was a sheepish unease between them now. Tom had been muttering words of encouragement softly under his breath up to this point, then he turned his head away from Bryan as if regretful of the love act. Bryan leaned over Tom in an attempt to have his own passion satisfied, but Tom lay they're removed and remote from the yearnings of Bryan. In desperation, Bryan dashed out of the room and into his own bedroom covering his own erection in case his mother was to see him. Once in his bedroom he sat down on his bed and brought himself to a climax almost immediately. There was no heightened delirious pleasure from his act, just a dull depressing feeling as a result. He suddenly became aware of his mother's voice calling upstairs.

'Are you two all right? There's a lot of activity going on up there. Breakfast is nearly ready.'

He lay back on his bed for a moment mulling over the situation he had got himself into. Tom was not gay. He would have responded to his advances if he were. God, what a mess he had made of this visit. How he longed to have Tom in his arms though. Why would he let him do what he had done if he didn't like it though? Maybe there was a chance that Tom was just scared to return his love for him. Maybe he had not had the same feelings as he had for another man before, and this was his first taste of gay love for him, and didn't quite know how to handle it. Maybe he should give him time.

CHAPTER 9

Doug's first week working with Dick seemed to drag. He had dreaded going back to his room at Mrs Dobson's and his relationship with Dick was not as he had hoped for. He knew Dick had a preference for other men, but he had shown no signs of showing this with him. Maybe it was the pressure of work that had restricted Dick in making moves to warm to him. There had been a moment when they were both at the side of the printing press trying to fathom out a problem. Their bodies had touched and Dick had placed an arm across his shoulders as they both peered down at the machine, and Dick had placed his head close to his as he shouted over the noise of other presses running. He had felt the warmth of Dick's breath against his ear, and as he turned to look up at Dick, just for a moment he thought Dick was going to offer him a kiss on the side of his face. How he wanted to be in contact with Dick. He had often found himself being aroused as he watched Dick walking down the print shop with his shirt off. That body of his was just waiting to be held and caressed. Maybe it was the heat in the oppressive workshop that was making him feel horny for his boss. When work was over at the end of the day he tried to pass the time drinking in the public houses. He had sat there for many an hour watching the men, mainly older than him, getting drunk and falling about. It was far from the scene he wanted or indeed the scene where he was likely to find another for a relationship. Somehow he couldn't bring himself to accept that he was a homosexual, as all he wanted was to have a warm loving relationship with another man. The law strictly forbade homosexual acts and so the gay scene had gone underground. If he wanted to find someone, he had to find the places where they socialised. Many a night he had laid there on his bed pondering over his situation. He didn't want sex with anyone; he wanted to be loved and to give love. He should never have left home. His thoughts flashed back to Bryan and the scene at the station as he was departing for London. He could feel Bryan's arms around him as they had embraced there on the platform. He knew that he had made a mistake in coming to London.

It was the Thursday of his second week of working with Dick when the call came. He was running one of the smaller presses at the time. He felt a tap on his shoulder.

'There's a phone call for you in the office,' Dick called out.

'A phone call?' Doug asked, his body suddenly beginning to tremble a little.

'Yes. I'll take over the press. You can take it in the office.'

He hurried towards the office wiping the ink from his hands with a rag. Closing the door behind him so as to cut out the noise of the printing presses, he picked up the phone.

'Hello. Who's calling?' His voice was warbling a little. He was not used to speaking on the phone.

'It's me, Bryan,' he heard the voice at the other end say. It sounded a long way away.

He had to sit down on the edge of the desk for support. He felt himself sweating, and brushed his forehead with his wrist. God, why was he so nervous?

'Hello. It's nice to hear from you. How are you?'

'Oh, I'm fine. And you?'

'Not enjoying London.'

'Pardon.'

'I said, I'm not enjoying London.

'When are you coming home for a break then?' Bryan asked.

'I don't know. If the job doesn't get any better, I might come home for good.'

Bryan's heart jumped a little on hearing this, for his week had not gone too well for him either either. They talked a little, but the conversation did not flow easily. The office door opened suddenly. Doug looked at the face of Dick. It was obvious that he been on the phone longer than he should have, and anyway, he couldn't continue the conversation with Dick in the office.

'Look. I'll give my mum a phone call as soon as I have sorted my mind out. Speak to you soon,' Doug said, bringing the conversation to an end. He placed the phone down and looked at Dick who was trying to look as if he had a purpose for his intrusion.

'I'm sorry I took so long on the phone,' Doug said.

'Was there a problem?' Dick asked.

'No not really. Just a friend keeping in touch.'

'You must be lonely down here in London. We haven't really had time to talk. It's my fault. Can I take you for a drink tonight after work?'

That would be nice,' Doug replied. His heart seemed to miss a beat on hearing this.

'I have a private club that I go to. Would you like to come along and meet others?' Dick asked.

'Others. What did he mean by- *others* ?

Six o'clock saw the two of them closing down the presses and washing the days grime away in the chipped earthenware sink at the back of the print shop. Doug felt a change in Dick's attitude as they stood side by side scrubbing their hands and arms free of the printing solvents that seemed to linger on their bodies as well, it was not a pleasant smell to have lingering about. Somehow the mood of Dick seemed to lighten. He gave a nudge with his thigh against Doug's as they scrubbed away at the sink. They looked at each other as if to say *I want to make contact with you.* Maybe Dick wanted to return to their teenage antics. Doug hoped so. As they stood there sharing the towel to dry their hands, their eyes met. Doug suddenly felt the urge to kiss those lips he had studied for the past few days. They had seemed so distant until now. With his heart beating at a fast pace as he reached out with his hand and placed it around Dick's head pulling them together. Dick didn't resist his attempt to kiss him. At first their lips met and there was a tentative nip of a kiss shared.

He couldn't remember ever having a feeling like this before. They embraced with their hands searching each other, as their kissing grew more intense. It was amazingly exciting that within those few moments of passion they searched each other for more pleasurable exchanges. Doug heard the moans of pleasure from Dick as his kisses rained down Dick's now naked body. Not once did either bother as to how their clothes were removed and scattered onto the print room floor. He had hoped for a more romantic scene than this for his return to lovemaking. He was completely under the control of his seducer now. Moments later Dick had pleasured him. He opened his eyes and found himself staring down at Dick.

'God you are so beautiful,' Dick was heard to say.' Let's not make love together in this dump of a place. I've wait too long for this moment, and I just want it to be right.'

For a moment he was tempted to beg for more attention. His heart was pounding faster and his head was about to explode. He felt Dick pat his erection as he started to move away from him. For a moment, they just stood eyeing each other.

'Oh God, I wanted you to make love to me so much,' he said. 'But you are right, this is not the right place.'

'Wait until you see where I'm taking you this evening,' Dick smiled.

'I was beginning to think that you had changed your ways and you were not interested in me any more. You have no idea how frustrated I been since coming down to London.'

'And I had been thinking the same. I guess it was that phone call you had that made me think harder about you, and what I was missing. Was that your boyfriend you were talking to?'

Doug smiled at the thought, then shook his head. But in his mind he really wanted to say more about Bryan back home. As they made there way to their separate rooms, Doug was beginning to feel excited about the evening ahead. They had parted with a kiss in the doorway of a shop for fear of being seen. It was a stupid bloody world they lived in. Why were they not able to show their love for each other apart from in private? Dick had arranged to call and meet him at his digs at seven o'clock. He washed and changed into his best things, and all the time he kept checking his watch. As it got closer to seven o'clock the excitement building up inside him was becoming almost unbearable. Not wanting Dick to have to knock at the front door and arousing Mrs Dobson's curiosity, he tiptoed his way past her door. Closing the front door behind him he walked a few paces up the road and sat down on a wall to wait for him. He hadn't to wait for long before he saw the swagger of a walk coming through the patches of dimly lit street lamps. He walked towards Dick and they greeted each other in the shadows. There was a brief embrace and a kiss shared before they walk their way into the streets of Kensington. Although they walked shoulder to shoulder they felt on edge for being seen. Even as their hands touched at times, they were aware that they might be seen. It was with some relief when Dick pointed ahead of them.

'Nearly there. That's the place up there on the right. See that white building on the corner, well it's the house next to it.'

Doug gave a sigh of relief as they started to climb the steps to the house, yet he suddenly began to feel nervous. What was he getting into? He only wanted to be with Dick. He stood back as Dick rang the doorbell. There was a sound of movement the other side of the door. A face appeared through the half open door.

'Hello Dick my friend. Glad you could make it. I see you have your friend with you. Good. Come on in. We have quite a party going on upstairs.'

Doug could feel the eyes of the host weighing him up as Dick ushered him inside the dimly lit hallway ahead of him.

'This is Doug,' Dick said as he introduced him.

'I'm Roger. How lovely to see such a sweet young man joining us this evening. Where on earth did you find such a charming young man Dick?'

'Take no notice of Roger Doug, he's like this with everyone,' Dick said, pushing past Roger as he spoke. 'Come on in and meet everyone.'

Doug could hardly walk the length of the hall for nerves. Dick opened a door at the end of the hall and entered a room that buzzed with people. Doug tried to focus on the faces around him. The room suddenly went quiet, and all heads turned towards Doug. He felt very exposed standing there.

'This is Doug. He's an old friend of mine. I mean a *young* friend of mine that I have known for a long time,' Dick said, turning to take hold of Doug's hand as he spoke and looking at him with a look of pride.

There were a few smiles that crept across the faces of the men in the some what crowded room. A few of the gathering made an effort to greet him with the odd wink or wave of a limp wrist. These were the dandies that Doug had heard about that met in secret for fear of arrest.

'Come, my dear boy, let me offer you a drink,' Roger suddenly said, leading Doug through the room to a table laden with an array of drinks and delicately cut sandwiches. Doug dragged Dick along with him by the hand. He could feel Dick squeezing his hand in assurance that he was there at his side. Roger handed both of them a glass of wine, then hurried away to join a young man at the far end of the room. Doug sipped at his wine and studied the scene. Although there were small groups of men standing around talking and laughing together, it was obvious that they were paired off. As he peered through the dimness of the room, he became aware that the large double doors at the far end of the room opened and shut as couples entered. Dick smiled at Doug's expression as he watched the scene.

'What goes on out there?' Doug asked.

Dick pulled him closer to him as he whispered in his ear, then kissed him. He felt Dick's hand searching around his arse. At first he felt embarrassed by this, yet had yearned for the feel of Dick's hands on him. There was a movement in his groin as he warmed to Dick's attention.

'We can go through those doors later if you want,' Dick whispered again.

Doug had seen most of the others in the room responding to the attention they giving to each other, so without thinking about the company he was in, he turned and placed his lips against Dick's and they kissed. At first it was no more than just a kiss. Dick took hold of Doug's glass of wine and placed it back on the table before he made his move to heighten the mood of their evening. Soon they were standing entwined in each other's arms with their hands frantically searching each other's bodies. They could hear some of the remarks and cheers from onlookers as they kissed now with passion. They writhed and pressed their erections together without fear of being seen doing so.

Dick suddenly eased himself free of the fevered passionate actions of Doug. Then, taking his hand, he led him through the admiring onlookers, and out through the double doors, closing them behind them. Doug blinked his eyes as he viewed the scene before him. They were standing in a large room with alcoves heaving with naked and partly dressed couples interlocked in sexual acts. He couldn't believe what he was seeing. Dick tugged at his hand and led him towards a winding staircase leading upstairs to a balcony. Doug couldn't help but look down into the dimly lit room below to double check the scene below. What was he getting himself into? On the landing he could make out several doors. He watched Dick as he went about checking to see if they were vacant. He tried two doors only to find that they were locked. The third door opened and he turned beckoning Doug to follow him. Doug's heart was beating fast now as he approached the room. It was obvious that Dick was familiar in the surroundings as he began to strike a match to light a candle. He must have used this room before else how would he know where to find the candle in the darkness? As the candlelight began to brighten, Doug could make out the double bed across the room. He quite expected to find writhing bodies dotted around, but at last they were alone. Dick sat down on the edge of the bed and reached out his arms for Doug to join him. He hesitated for a moment.

'Can I lock the door?' Doug asked.

Dick gave a hint of a laugh, stood up again and went back to the door and turned the lock.

'There,' Dick said, as he started to remove his jacket.

Doug stood there not quite knowing how to act. He had never been in a situation like this before, and he felt nervous.

CHAPTER 10

It was Friday, and it had been a tense week for Bryan so far. Tom seemed to not want to respond to the advances that Bryan had been making, and although Tom had not rejected the love acts that he was receiving from Bryan nightly, be had not returned the love act. This was getting at Bryan, and he was becoming frustrated and desperate for Tom's love. Today was the last day of Tom's visit, and as frustrated as he was, in a way he was beginning to almost welcome Saturday coming around. At least it would put a stop to the pain that racked his body and an end to his desperate attempts for Tom's returned love. He lay there in bed listening to his mother preparing breakfast downstairs. The sun was streaming through his bedroom window now, yet he was not looking forward to getting out of bed and facing the day. Suddenly he heard Tom's door across the landing being opened and shut. He listened as he heard Tom's footsteps along the landing as he made his way to the bathroom. This morning though he didn't feel the pangs of pain in the pit of his stomach as usual when hearing Tom's movement. This morning he had no urge to get up out of bed to take catch sight of him, naked, apart from a towel around his waist. It wasn't that he was not in love with Tom now, it was that he was feeling exhausted with past attempts to receive Tom's love. He knew that as soon as he caught sight of Tom's beautiful body, he would be yearning to caress and hold him in his arms. He remained in bed curled up with one of his pillows in his arms. The thought of having to go through another day of rejection. There was a knock on his door. It was his mother bringing him his early morning cup of tea. He hurriedly uncurled himself from his pillow and began sitting up in bed to receive her.

'Come in,' he called out.

The door opened and he could hear the cup a saucer rattling in her unsteady hand.

'Good morning darling. Did you sleep well?'

'Quite well,' he lied.

'Shall I leave you to take Tom's tea into him?'

'Could you take it in to him please this morning,' he asked.

His mother placed his tea down on the bedside table and glanced at him.

'Is there anything wrong between you two?' she asked.

His mother was a cagey old thing. He had a feeling that she knew more than she let on about life.

'Not really.'

'What does that mean then?'

'Nothing.'

'Well I'll leave you to drink your tea. Breakfast is nearly ready.'

With that, she turned and left the room carrying Tom's tea on the tray. He heard her saying something to Tom as she closed the door. He tried to catch what they were saying, but the opening and closing of doors drowned their conversation. Even the sound of Tom's voice sent tremors down his spine. For Christ sake, what was wrong with him? Surely he should not have feelings like this all the time. Was this what love was all about? Was being gay, and in love, any different to the love of heterosexuals? Was he destined to suffer a life of pain and suffering for being born this way? Was this God's way of making him see the errors of his ways? He took a mouthful of tea and suddenly felt quite sick in the pit of his stomach. He lay down again to collect himself. After a while he came to terms with the fact that he had to face the world again. He made sure that he made enough noise in opening and closing his bedroom door and repeated this act with the bathroom door as well. He had hoped that Tom would have popped his head out of his room with a greeting.

After washing himself and dressing, he made his way downstairs for breakfast. Tom was already sitting down at the table. He looked up and gave half a smile to him.

'Morning. Did you sleep well?'

'Not bad,' Tom replied.

'What about you?' his mother asked.

'About the same,' he said, looking at Tom across the table.

There was tenseness in the air, and the conversation was quite stunted. Breakfast was placed in front of both of them, and they ate in silence.

'What are you two up to today?' Bryan's mum asked.

Bryan and Tom looked up from their eating as if to ask themselves the question.

'Well. As it's my last day here, I'd like to go into the village and take a look around,' Tom said.

'Are you going to come with me?' he asked, looking at Bryan across the table.

'I think I'll just catch up on some sun bathing. It looks like being a nice day again,' Bryan replied.

'Is there a problem between you two?' mum asked. 'You seem to be very off with each other.'

The two looked at each other searching for a reaction. Bryan gave half a smile as if to make things better between them, but Tom just remained bland. Then suddenly he gave a cough as if to clear his throat before speaking. Then as he pushed his chair away from the table he looked at Bryan.

'It's me. I'm sorry. I haven't been very good company this week. I'm sorry. I think I'm still sorting life out in my head,' he said. As he spoke both mum and Bryan could see tears of emotion starting to appear in Tom's eyes. Mum made a move to comfort him with her arm around his shoulders.

'Bloody war,' she uttered.

Tom kissed her on her cheek and struggled to move away. Bryan sat there not quite knowing what to do. He wanted to be the one with his arms around Tom, but that would have been a give-away to his mother. He knew that he couldn't comfort Tom with just a hug. He would have wanted to kiss him as well and show his love for him. How could he do that in front of his mother? Men don't do things like that. He just sat there watching Tom leave the kitchen and head upstairs. He could feel his mother's eyes on him now. It was a tense moment. Getting up from the table he hurried out of the kitchen in pursuit of Tom. He found him in his room sitting on the side of his bed sobbing. Bryan shut the door and sat down at Tom's side. He placed his arms around Tom to comfort him.

'Come on mate, don't crack up like that. Come on.'

Tom laid his head on Bryan's shoulder. He sniffed and reached inside his trouser pocket for his handkerchief. He sat up again and blew his nose and wiped his eyes.

'What a fucking idiot I've been,' he said.

'No you haven't,' Bryan said, comforting him again with a hug. 'We have been through some tough times. Bloody war.'

'You know it's not that,' Tom said, suddenly standing up from the bed.

Bryan remained silent as he watched Tom stroll across the room to stare out of the window. It seemed ages before Bryan could bring himself to join him. They stood there staring out across the meadows at the foot of the garden. The sound of the river flowing drifted up through the open window. It made for sweet music that helped calm the moment.

'I want to go into the village to buy some flowers for your mother.'
Come with me,' Tom asked.

Bryan planted a kiss on the side of Tom's cheek before turning to go
to his own room to put on a shirt. As he turned, Tom held him by
the shoulders and looked deep into his eyes. For a moment their lips
touched, but almost as quickly as Tom had made the move, he drew
away again. Bryan left the room in a daze. What did he have to do
to get Tom to give himself to him? He knew that he wanted to, but
something was holding him back. In his room he hurriedly pulled
his shirt on and brushed his hair. He stared at his face in the mirror.
He looked flushed. There was a tap on his door.

'Are you coming with me?' he heard Tom ask.

The village was not far away so that they didn't have to find long
topics of conversation. He felt that Tom wanted to say something of
importance as they walked through the lanes. Something was holding
him back from relating to him. What was it? He was the one that had
made all the moves to show he loved and cared for Tom. And Tom
had never once refused his attempts to made love to him. He had just
given himself to him, and as soon as his love juices had been released,
he clammed up again into his shell. Not once had he returned his love.
How he had longed to feel Tom's hands searching deep into his thighs
with returned love. Even as they kissed, it always just remained as
a gentle touching of lips. How he wished to feel Tom's passionate
searching tongue deep down into his throat. Maybe Tom was not gay
after all, and he had just gone along with his fumbling wandering
hands and kisses just to please him. But surely he would have to be
gay to allow him to make love to him like that?

'You're deep in thought again,' Tom suddenly said, bring him out of his confusion.

'Sorry.'

They smiled at each other. It was a welcome relief when they found themselves in the village- square at last. There were very few shops or shoppers. The florist was just a small shop crammed into the corner of the small post office. Bryan decided to stay outside so as not to have to converse with inquiring villagers. As he waited for Tom to buy the flowers, he looked across to the pub across the road. Memories of that meeting he had with Doug flooded back to him. He wondered what he was up to and how he was getting on in London now. Tom suddenly broke his thoughts as he jokingly displayed the flowers he had purchased for his mother.

'She will love those. You shouldn't have,' Bryan said, admiring the spray of flowers.

'I should have. Your mother is a lovely woman to have put up with me for a whole week.'

'Fancy a beer?' Bryan asked.

They crossed the road and Tom sat down on the bench seat while Bryan bought the beers from inside the pub. On his return, Tom moved himself and his flowers along the table to make room. He gave a laugh at the way a few other drinkers sitting around them watched their every move.

'People will be talking about us, what with the flowers and all,' Tom giggled.

'I wish it were true,' Bryan quickly replied.

'What?'

'That you were showing your love for me with flowers.'

The words just seemed to have been stored up inside him and had suddenly found the moment to express his emotions. He watched Tom's reactions. His head dropped down as he glanced down at the ground searching for an escape route. Bryan took a sip of his beer before he continued.

'I'm sorry if I have made a fool of myself this week. I can't help it if I love you,' Bryan said. 'I only wish you loved me in the same way.'

Tom remained silent as he listened to Bryan's whispered words in case he was over heard. Tom started to look up. Then sipping his beer and wiping the froth away from his lips with the back of his hand, he faulted for words.

'You have to give me time.'

Bryan felt a tingling sensation running down his spine. At least Tom was not rejecting his love.

Why couldn't they show their feelings for each other in public? Why didn't people think that people like him have feelings? There was a feeling of desperation running through his body now.

There was so little time left before Tom went home. And what then? Maybe he would not see him again and he would never know what it was like to receive his love. He thought on Tom's reply.

'I understand. Sure, I know I have rushed into love with you,' he said, realising that his voice was getting louder, and people on the next table were glancing across at the two of them. But somehow he was far from caring now. They remained silent sipping at their beer until their glasses were empty. All eyes were on them as they began to leave the pub and make their way home, the flowers adding to the curious onlookers. Bryan wanted to continue the talking about his feelings for Tom, but knew that it would not ease the situation. Once they were out of view of the village they walked with arms around each other and suddenly the world seem a brighter place for Bryan. They arrived back at the cottage and entered the kitchen. Tom handed Bryan's mother the flowers and there was an emotional scene for a few moments, for she was not used to being treated like this since her husband had died. Bryan watched as her face lit up with joy as she hunted for a vase to put them in.

After a small lunch the two of them made their excuses and without discussion as to what they were going to do for the rest of the day, they left the cottage and headed for the meadows. The sun was at the height of the day now as they made their way through the long grass. Once out of sight of the cottage they felt free to relate to each other again. They could see for what seemed miles across the Cambridge flat countryside that was shaped only by the lines of trees and hedgerow that divided the boundaries of each farm. They had walked at least a mile with arms linked around each other's shoulders, and heads resting together as lovers do. They were free to relate to each other without fear of being seen by society. They made a small clearing by treading down the tall grasses and lay down together. With shirts removed and the sun baring down on their nakedness, they felt relaxed for the first time together that week. They embraced and kissed now with a passion that had been so restricted during the week for fear of being caught, for here they were alone and free under the sun and clear blue sky. They paused for air and laughed a nervous laugh together for they knew that this was a new stage in their relationship. They had spoken few words up to this point, but now they were feeling more relaxed as they lay facing one another with heads resting on each other's outstretched arms they began to find the words that had evaded them all week.

'I'll miss you when you go home tomorrow,' Bryan said, searching Tom's eyes for a reaction.

''I don't want to leave either,' Tom replied.

There was a brief pause in their conversation. Bryan reached out and placed his hand across Tom's chest. Tom smiled as he felt fingertips teasing his nipples for a second, then nothing. Bryan searched into Tom's eyes for reactions, and for the first time, Tom responded by reaching out to tease his lover's nipples in return. He felt a shudder run through Bryan's body as he teased them to a hard. They leaned their heads closer and felt their breath on each other's lips. They shared a gentle touching of lips as their heads rested close together and their eyes continued to searching.

'I thought I had offended you,' Bryan said, his voice in a whisper.

''Why do you say that?'

'Because I made love to you, and I wasn't sure that you wanted my love.'

Bryan felt Tom's short intake of breath as he made to gesture with a snore of a laugh.

'I was far from offended, I have never had that done to me before. You see, I had never thought that I could never receive the love of a man, but it was wonderful.'

'But why didn't you return my love?' Bryan asked, drawing his head slightly away from Tom's and searching for answers.

'I don't know. I so wanted to, but it seemed wrong in the cottage. I felt a little insecure I think.'

'But you let me make love to you.'

'Yes. And each time you left my room, I cried for my own insecurity. Fuck, how I wanted to return your love. How I wanted you to get into bed with me and make love…and…you know.'

Bryan felt a lump swell in his throat. He leaned forward and kissed Tom again and again.

'I thought all the time I was making love to you that you were not wanting me to do so. I have been a wreck lying in my bed afterwards each night.

They cradled each other in their arms and their hands started to explore each other. Tom drew Bryan closer to him. He was erect and hard as he pushed himself against Bryan's erect shaft.

For a while they shared the joy of the moment with only their rough flannel trousers dividing their bodies. Both were waiting for the other to make the first move. Both their bodies were trembling with expectation. Tom was the first to make the move that unlocks the passions that situations like they were experiencing so memorable in later life. For both had read about scenes and acts of love, but now they were at those very crossroads. For now they were about to be released from those fears of being I love with another of their own sex. He rolled himself across and on top of Bryan. He leaned forward and ran both hands down the length of Bryan's bare body until he reached the waist of his trousers. He looked down at Bryan searching for reactions from him. He was greeted with and expression of pleasure and excitement as he started to remove his trousers. For a moment Tom looked down and stared at Bryan's erectness. Up till this time he had only held his own. He listened to the moans and expectations from Bryan as he lay there on his back, so naked, so beautiful. Moments later those moans were of joyous delight at his lover's tender care in reaching a climax. They had waited for this moment of gay love right through their teen years up until the age of twenty three.

How he was able to contain himself and hold back, he had no idea. He reached out for Tom's erection and felt Tom shudder at his hold. They pleased each other this way, so free and naked under the sun. They began to reach the beginning of those sensations that would bring them to a climax. Tom suddenly lurched back to arch his back, and at the same time grasped hold of Bryan's shaft so as he had both love rods under his control. He worked away until the moment that they both called out with joy as they erupted in unison. It was explosive, and it took a while for the moment to subside before they collapsed in each other's arms raining kisses on each other.

'Thank God for that,' Tom said his voice full of emotion. 'Oh how I have wanted for this moment.'

'Me too,' Bryan managed to say between kisses.

They laughed and talked words of affection for each other as they lay in each other's arms. Soon their excitement, almost exhausted, found them drifting asleep. They had slept there in the tall grass for while when Tom felt a tingling sensation on his nose. He put his hand to his face and the tingle stopped for a moment. Then it returned. His hand reached out again and he squinted one eye open only to find a smiling Bryan teasing him with a blade of grass. Bryan had been awake for a while studying his lovers nakedness. How could it be wrong to love such beauty? He wanted to shout aloud his love, but then nobody would hear him or understand.

'How long have you been studying me?' Tom asked, opening his eyes and smiling at the question.

'I was just thinking how we had wasted our time this week. I feel sad that you are going home tomorrow,' Bryan said, reaching out to touch Tom's lips with his fingertips. He smiled as Tom kissed them in return. ' Do you want to go all the way?'

The question made Tom suddenly perch himself up on his elbow at the thought. He felt that he was being put under pressure on the last day of his holiday with Bryan. Surely they couldn't just do it like that? Well he couldn't anyway; he needed time, and had to be in the right mood, for he was entering into something that was not to be taken lightly. What they had just done together so far was quite innocent, but to actually fuck, or be fucked, was to commit fully to a lifestyle that was forbidden by law. All these thoughts ran riot through his head. He looked at Bryan who had been studying him lying there deep in thought.

'I don't know. I'm not sure about us getting too involved. I'm not sure I can do it.'

Bryan felt deflated at Tom's reply.

They both lay on their backs with hands linked behind their heads staring up into the clear blue sky.

The sun was now at its peak making Bryan feel quite horny at his exposed nakedness under it. Tom, on seeing the stirring in Bryan's loins made to stand up.

'I want to take a leak,' he said, as he turned to walk away from the clearing they had made.

Bryan watched as Tom made his way through the long grass to stand with his back to him as he attended to nature. His hand went down to comfort his now rising penis. He lay there staring at the pert arse of Tom. How he wished that Tom had wanted to make love there and then. But, he was glad that they had ventured with their love making to this stage at least. How the week had been wasted. To rush Tom into completing the act now would be wrong, for to do so might ruin things forever. Tom was now returning. He raised his hands above his head and gave a little gig like movements of his hips as he walked back through the long grass. He stood above Bryan, legs apart, and looked down on his arousal. It would have been so easy to be tempted to complete the act there and then, but something was holding him back. Bryan, sensing that he was putting pressure on the relationship, stood up and gathered his clothes.

'I think I'm going for a swim to cool myself down. Oh God, you don't know how I want to do it with you,' Bryan said.

'So I see,' Tom laughed, looking down at Bryan's reducing erection. 'Come on, I'll take you up on that swim.'

They ran through the long grass naked and feeling free. They laughed as they playfully tried to trip each other up. These moments were so far removed from the horror times in the trenches in France.

The water was cool as they waded into the flowing river. They swam towards the willow tree, stopping only to playfully turn on the other to give a ducking. Breathlessly they clambered up onto the tree trunk and sat there laughing together. It was sometime before they really spoke.

'Does your mother know about you?' Tom asked suddenly.

'Oh God no. I'm dreading telling her. How about your parents?'

'They have no idea. But then I wasn't at all sure until I came down here to be seduced by you.'

They laughed at the statement. They had been sitting apart but Bryan reached out and put his arm around Tom, and they sat there in silence again.

'Did you mind me making love to you this week?' Bryan asked.

Tom shook his head.

'Didn't you want to do it to me as well?'

'I don't know what I felt. I just know I liked what you were doing for me.'

'But you haven't answered my question.'

'I just felt unsure that I could do it. You see I never thought that was what I was coming on holiday for. I had never thought of having sex with another bloke before this. I really didn't know how to handle it all.'

Bryan laughed aloud at the way this sounded.

'You know what I mean. You see, not much goes on in Norfolk.'

'Well I thought you handled it well this afternoon,' Bryan added.

Tom suddenly heaved his elbow out and pushed Bryan backward into the water. He watched as Bryan sputtered his way the surface.

'Serves you right you little seducer,' Tom laughed.

After leaving the river they headed back through the meadow. As they came in sight of the cottage again, they stopped to put their clothes on. Suddenly the mood changed, for it dawned on them that they had just experienced a passage of their lives that would change them forever. They could see Bryan's mother watching their every move through the kitchen window. Now they would have to act as if they were just good friends and not lovers.

'You've been away ages. And look at you both you're covered in grass. Whatever have you been up to?'

They both looked at each other and laughed as they went back outside into the garden to brush themselves down their every move was being watched once again.

'Do you think your mother knows about us?' Tom suddenly asked, glancing back to the kitchen window and back to Bryan again.

'I don't know. But I have a feeling that she has a good idea.'

'Are you going to tell her?'

Bryan finished brushing himself down and then turned to Tom as he tried to remove grass from his own clothes. As he started picking the odd piece of grass off Tom's shirt he could feel his mothers eyes watching his every move. Tom remained still for him.

'You haven't answered my question,' Tom whispered over his shoulder.

'I really don't know. It would break her heart.'

They went indoors and sat at the kitchen table once again. Bryan looked at his mother as she poured tea from the teapot into their mugs. How could he tell her that he was gay?

'There you are. I expect you could do with that,' she said as she placed the mugs down on the table.

'Thanks,' Tom said, looking down at his tea then up across the table at Bryan.

Bryan cradled his mug of tea in his hands as he stared dreamily back at Tom. Although he had searched into his eyes many times over the past week he had never really studied how blue they were or the length of his eyelashes. He had beautiful features. They smiled at each other across the table and their bare feet touched and played in private underneath. God, he was falling for Tom in a big way. All he wanted to do was to take him away and make love to him, but how and where?

That evening they spent their time lounging and reading by the range in the kitchen. Mother made her exit to bed dead on ten o'clock as usual. They both sat there waiting for the sound of her bedroom door closing before they could relax. They tested the silence until they were sure mother was settled in bed. Bryan reached out his hand to Tom and they sat there for a while content in each other's company. Bryan tried to read on, but he was not really focusing on the words.

'I'm ready for bed, 'Tom suddenly said.

Bryan knew that this was going to be the testing point. It was their last night together. His heart was beginning to race as he closed his book.

'You go on up while I lock up down here,' Bryan said.

As he checked around the cottage he could hear Tom's whereabouts. They had not said goodnight to each other, as they knew that they were going to be with each other that night. They passed each other on the landing and for a brief moment embraced and kissed in silence. As Bryan finished in the bathroom and turned the light off, he could see that Tom had left his door slightly open. Was this the invite that he was so looking for? He slowly opened the door and entered.

'I couldn't go to sleep without saying goodnight,' Bryan said.

Tom lay there in bed with the bedclothes exposing his bare chest. He patted the vacant side of his bed with his hand. Bryan looked at the expression on Tom's face. Tom was making it impossible to ignore the invite to climb in bed with him, not that he wanted asking twice. He closed the door behind him and turned the lock, then began to remove his clothes hurriedly. Tom pulled the bedclothes to one side for him to climb in bed next to him. Soon they were in each other's arms.

They kissed with a feverish passion and their hands searched each other body. Bryan sighed a sigh of ecstasy as Tom ran his kisses down his body in search of his nipples. For a while he lay there feeling them being kissed and teased, a sensation that drove him to the heights of delirium. They explored every inch of each other's bodies as they embraced and entwined themselves across the bed. Their minds were racing away as the time for their virginity's to be taken drew nearer. The bedclothes had been removed in their passionate manoeuvres and Bryan found himself on top of Tom when that moment came where they were ready to commit themselves to one another. For a while he lay there as Tom stroked his erection with calm caressing tenderness and then brought his own hardness into his hold, just like it had been in the meadow that afternoon. Just for a while he poised himself above Tom to enjoy the sensation of their two cocks being worked as one as before. The feel of their two cocks, so firm and ready, almost tempted him to enjoy the experience once again to the climax, but he wanted to experience more than this. With his fingers searching for the warmth of Tom's anus, and he began to tease the rim. Tom groaned at the first entry and his body reacted with a shudder. As he began to excite Tom in readiness to be entered, Tom was muttering.

'Not now Bryan. I can't do it here.'

Bryan had only heard faint mutterings, but not coherent words. He began to increase his attempts to tease the love rim and to experience his own dreams of making Tom happy, but Tom had tensed himself and became motionless with his own loving. Bryan was frustrated now.

'What's the matter?' he asked, sitting back on his haunches and looking down at Tom.

'I want you to make love to me so much, but this is not the right time and place.'

Bryan could see the unhappiness in Tom's face. His frustrations turned to understanding. He lowered himself down onto Tom and kissed him. He felt Tom's arms embraced him. They lay there motionless for a while, with bodies trembling with their emotional state. Bryan looked into his eyes and then kissed Tom gently on the lips again.

'I love you too much to make you want to have me,' Bryan said.

'I'm so sorry. I'm scared I think. Scared that I might loose you, and scared of what it's like.'

'Scared. I don't think you should be scared. I would want you to give yourself to me, trust me, and enjoy the love I have for you. I would not hurt you. So why not tonight?'

'It's not you. It's me. Maybe it's knowing that men aren't supposed to love each other this way. And I think it's because I fear your mother is listening for our every move.'

Bryan rolled himself off of Tom and lay by his side. He began to realise that he was to blame. He had pushed Tom into something before he was ready. But how long did he have to wait for Tom's love? He turned on his side to face Tom. Then reaching out his hand he ran his hand down Tom's taunt body, patted his now flaccid penis, and made to get out of bed. Tom reached out and a grasped his arm in an attempt to hold him back.

'It's best that I go back to my own bed,' Bryan said, collecting his clothes from the floor in a bundle. He looked down at Tom again. He looked distressed and unhappy. He leaned forward again and placed a gentle kiss on Tom's cheek. He tasted the saltiness of a tear. Then, unlocking the door he left Tom's room to enter his. He gave a glance down the landing towards his mother's room. He could see her light on through the gap under the door. Closing his door gently, he climbed into bed and lay there in cold silence and with his body still tense with expectation. He was not sure how long he had been asleep when he heard his door being opened. He must have been asleep though as his eyes were trying hard to open. He quite expected to hear his mother's voice as she brought him his early morning tea in bed, but as the room was still in darkness. As he went turn over to look towards the door, he felt the bed move and the bedclothes being drawn back.

'Did I wake you?' It was Tom. 'I couldn't sleep,' he said, as his body slid between the sheets and snuggled his naked body up close to Bryan.

CHAPTER 11

Standing together on the station platform waiting for Tom's train to arrive drained them of conversation. They had taken it in turns to carry his travel case down through the lanes, and they had made good time as they had twenty minutes wait for the train. They felt that the whole world was watching them, as they stood there motionless. Tom suddenly dragged his case towards the bike shed. No one was around, and they were a little more private now. Tom took Bryan by his shoulders and squarely placed him against the side of the shed. They kissed in secret.

'I'm going to miss you so much,' Bryan eventually said.

'I'll miss you too. It's been a lovely week. And I'm only sorry that I took so long to come around to admitting that I wanted your love. I'm so sorry.'

'Sorry for what?'

'Well for waiting till yesterday. I will never forget making love to you in the meadow.'

Bryan smiled as Tom went on talking. He placed a finger on Tom's lips, and he was silent.

'I don't regret a thing,' Bryan said.

He paused, as Tom wanted to speak again.

'I don't regret not going all the way with you last night. I just want it to be at the right time and place, a place where I can give myself freely to you. Oh God, how I wish I could have given myself to you last night.'

'I know. I understand. I'm just so happy that we were able to be together as we were. I don't want you just to fuck you, I want you for who you are,' Bryan said, his voice full of emotion. 'When will I see you again?'

'You have to come up to visit me. I know my parents are due to take a break in Blackpool soon. We would have the house to ourselves,' said Tom.

Bryan kissed him again as their bodies rested together against the shed. There was a sudden noise of a gate being opened and closed in a rather hurried way. They quickly parted and adjusted their clothing, which had been ruffled by their roaming hands. They walked casually onto the platform again just in time to see a young lad throwing his bike into the bike shed. The lad smiled at them as he hurried down the platform towards the ticket office. The train was due to arrive, and they stood there exposed to the public once again.

'Do you think he saw us?' Tom laughed.

'I don't think so. So your parents are off on holiday.'

'Yes. I'll write to you as soon as I get back. I know it's next month, but I'm not sure of the date.'

'Oh God, that would be bloody great,' Bryan said, turning his head as he heard the train approaching.

'You'll love the place. Not much goes on up there, but at least we will be on our own, ' Tom said, looking towards the oncoming train.

They stood there enveloped in clouds of smoke from the engine. Tom opened a carriage door and shoved his case inside. The carriage was empty. Then, turning towards Bryan, they embraced quickly before Tom climbed inside. He closed the door and leaned out of the window. Their hands touched as the train started to pull away.

'I'll write as soon as I get home. Thank your mother for the stay again. I love you.'

'I love you too,' Bryan called out over the noise of the train engine as it gained speed. He waved to Tom until he was out of sight. He walked home feeling emotionally drained yet excited about his coming stay with Tom in Norfolk. To think, a couple of weeks with him alone.

CHAPTER 12

—〰️ဿ〰️—

Doug strained his eyes to open. His head was thumping and his mouth raw and dry. He was lying on top of a bed with only a sheet pulled across his naked body. Where the hell was he? He made a move to raise his head off of the mattress but the room spun around with his efforts. Panic suddenly set in as he lay there. What had gone on last night? He eased himself up on his elbows and forced his eyelids to open. Resting his body against the headboard he glanced around as his eyes adjusted to the dimness of the room. All he could remember was entering the room with Dick. Where was Dick? He eased his legs off the bed and sat there trying to collect himself for a moment. He felt a dull ache in his groin and his hand went down automatically as if to check himself out. He had a vague idea what that feeling was, but how and why? His head started to clear a little as he tried to recollect the happenings of last evening. The door had been locked he remembered that. Dick had tempted him into bed with him, not that he needed much encouragement to do that. He vaguely remembered undressing and climbing into bed with Dick. Then there were the drinks that interrupted their passionate bouts of kissing. Where did those drinks come from? It must have been a pre arranged set up that Dick had drawn him into. Had they had sex? He couldn't remember much more than that, but their were the tell tale signs raging through the pit of his stomach, and his penis felt as though it had been over active. Sitting on the edge of the bed he tried to collect himself. His clothes were still on the chair where he had left them. Trying to stand up was not easy as his head was still swimming around and his legs were shaky. Pulling on his clothes and made for the door which he found unlocked. Where the hell was Dick? Nerves kicked in as he opened the door to see if anyone was around. The huge landing was strewn with odd garments of clothing, glasses, half- empty bottles of wine and gin. He could hear voices and laughter coming from a door partly open from across the landing. All he wanted to do was to get out of the building as fast as possible now.

He had taken less than a few steps when the door suddenly opened across the landing. A young man in his early twenties stood they're smiling at him. He was wearing nothing but his pants.

'Hello. What do I see here my lovely friends,' he called out to the crowd in the room behind him.

Doug froze to the spot, as suddenly there were half-clad men all trying to view their new recruit.

'Why don't you come in and join us,' the first man said.

Doug tried to ignore him as he started to continue his unstable walk down the landing.

'Oh. Look at him. He wants to go home. Mind you, he's had quite a full night,' the young man said.

There was laughter that followed that remark. Doug stopped in his tracks, turned and approached the ogling faces in the doorway.

'Where's Dick?' he demanded.

The doorway suddenly cleared of bodies as he was invited to view the scene inside the room. There was a lot of laughter as he partly entered the room. There was Dick, sitting up in bed resting his naked body against the headboard. He raised a glass of wine he was holding and the other hand was caressing a young man's equally naked body that was draped across him. He smiled at Doug.

'Did you sleep well darling?' Dick called out.

There was laughter that echoed the room. Doug just stood there frozen to the spot. Dick was in a state of stupor as he lay there on the bed. Doug quickly stared at the scene, then made his way out of the room feeling quite sick and scared at the thought of what he had got himself into. Had this rampant sex crazed group of gay men raped him? As he reached the door that led out to the staircase, he felt a hand grab his shoulder. He turned sharply, ready to defend himself this time.

'What the hell are you doing?' Doug demanded. 'Get your hand off of me.'

'Now hold on. I only wanted to speak to you.'

Doug stared at the young man and then made to go through the door.

'Can I tell you what happened last night?'

Doug stopped in his tracks. He was not sure that he wanted to hear.

'I rescued you from the initiation ceremony that all new members go through on their first night.'

'Member of what? I just came on an invited from Dick. What bloody membership?' Doug asked.

'Never mind. Look; come downstairs before they catch us together. My names James.'

Doug hurried through the door followed by James. He could feel his anger rising now. All he wanted was to get the hell out of there. As they reached the entrance hall, James once again placed his hand on Doug's shoulder. They stood by the front door facing each other. Doug was ready to fight James if he had to. James smiled at his anger and removed his hand away.

'You would be wise not to come back here again. Last night, as I was saying, I rescued you from the mob. They love new recruits.'

'I'm not a recruit.'

'Then you had no idea what you were here for then?'

'I wasn't here for an orgy. I came to a party at the invitation of Dick.'

James gave a slight snorting laugh at this statement.

'My dear friend. I guess it's your first visit to London. How long have you known Dick?'

'Too long I'm beginning to think. Look let me get out of this place.'

'Where are you going at this time of the day?' James asked.

It suddenly dawned on Doug that it was going to be difficult to get back into his lodging house. It was gone six o'clock in the morning. There was no way he could gain entrance to his room at this time of day. All he knew was that he had to get out of the house. He turned the lock of the front door and opened it. The welcoming fresh air of the early morning felt good. He breathed in deeply.

As he left the house and began to walk the streets, James followed close behind him. Doug stopped and turned to face him. If it was coming to the point where he had to fight his way free of James and his party of friends, then it was going to have to be now.

'Look. Will you leave me alone,' he said, standing his ground as James approached him.

'Not until you let me explain what happened to you last night and I'm sure that you are going to be alright,' James said. 'Look. How about a cup of tea at the market café up the road?'

Doug stood his ground facing James. Somehow his head was telling him to move away, yet his heart was telling him that wanted to know what had happened to him in that room.

'Oh come on. The café will be full of the market traders, so I don't think you'll have any trouble from them,' James said.

'Then why are you bothering to want to tell me about last night?'

'It's just that you don't look the same as the rest of them, and I've seen what goes on in that house.'

'Then tell me here, right here and now,' Doug demanded.

James pulled his coat collar up high around his neck. It was a cold damp morning. He stood there shifting from one foot to the other in an attempt to keep warm.

'Look. What harm are you going to come to by having a cup of tea in the café?'

Somehow he was beginning to quite nervous and cold. His anger had subsided, and he was beginning to shiver with the cold. He looked up the road where he could see the lights from the café in the distance. Then he looked at James again and nodded. He had no where else to go just yet.

The café was full, but the warmth and the smell of food being cooked seemed inviting. Doug took a look around him at the market workers laughing a chatting together. They were stocky thick set men who had worked in the market all of their lives. For a moment Doug began to feel out of place as many eyes followed the two of them around as they tried to find a table to sit at.

'Tea and anything to eat?' James asked.

'Just a tea. Thanks.'

He watched James as he stood at the counter across the other side of the café. He was warming to him, as he seemed a nice chap, but why would he want to follow him out of the house though and try to explain events of last night? He smiled to himself as he watched James standing there in his dandy clothes amongst the market porters in their overalls and white coats. How out of place they both were? But at least it was warm.

'Here you are then. One mug of tea,' James said, seating himself down at the table.

They sat there together a while in silence. Dough cupped his mug of tea in his hands to warm himself up. The tea tasted good.

'Why chase after me?' Doug suddenly asked, looking around to see if they were being listened to.

'It's just that I wanted to be sure that you were all right. I can remember my first time in that place. It's not a good place to be invited to. You were lucky,' James said, smiling across the small table.

'Lucky,' Doug exploded.

James looked around. He smiled as he placed a finger against his lips to hush Doug's voice.

'What do you think happened to you last night?' James asked, still keeping his finger to his lips.

'I don't know. All I know is that I was molested. I think I was fucked. In fact I know I was fucked. But how many times? And who doped me?' James asked. His voice croaked as he spoke.

'Look this isn't the best place to talk like this. Drink up and I'll take you to my place. It's only a short walk from here,' James said.

Doug shook his head. He was not going to go into another situation like last night. For Christ sake, was the whole of London like this? James watched Doug's expression. He smiled again.

'You'll be quite safe where I live. There's only me in the house as my partner left me weeks ago.'

With that, James stood up and looked down at Doug.

For a moment Doug froze in his chair. Yes, he was keen to learn what had happened to him during the night, yet in a way he wanted to get right away from the scene and run back home to Purr. James seemed a nice type, and after all he could always leave if James tried anything on with him. He looked at James standing there, and if he had been meeting him for the first time, he would have gladly taken up the offer to go home with him. He pushed his chair back and followed James out of the café. It had not been the right place to conduct their conversation in. James patted him on his shoulder as they walked the length of the street and towards his house.

'There. We are nearly there now. See the white-house at the end of the terrace,' James said, pointing ahead of them.

They climbed the steps up to the front door. Doug looked around him. How could James afford to live in a house like this? Once inside, James offered to take Doug's coat to hang up in the large square entrance hall. They entered the lounge with its large Indian rug, huge bay windows with heavy draped curtains. This house was the house of a wealthy man, Doug thought. He sat down in one of the well-arranged armchairs that surrounded the ornate white marble fireplace. He felt more secure sitting in the chair. James had asked him if he wanted a drink at all, but it was far too early in the morning for that. He settled for a glass of water. He was eager to learn of his fate last night.

James settled down in the chair opposite Doug. They sat there weighing each other up for a time. Doug was feeling edgy sitting there sipping his water. He suddenly felt the anger swelling up inside him. What was this all meaning by James bringing him here alone? Why should he suddenly trust James, for he might have escaped from one situation only to find that he was about to drift into another? At least with drinking water it was not likely to be doped like his drinks last night.

'How long have you known Dick?' James suddenly asked.

'Since I was a teenager. I was offered a job working with him, but we had not seen each other for a few years up until I came to London to work for him. How long have you known him then?'

'I don't really know him. I only know about him,' James replied.

'What do you mean by that then?'

'He's well known for his social life and his young men he surrounds himself with.'

Doug leaned forward in his chair wanting to hear more. Why was James telling him this?

'He tried it on me once, and like you I fell for his tricks. He uses Rogers house as a place to satisfy his sexual pleasures. You don't know how close you were to getting involved with his lot. You were close to being ravaged under the influence of drugs by more than one of them.'

'What about you then?' Doug asked.

'What about me?'

'Well why should you take the trouble to rescue me. And why do you go to that house anyway if you know it's like that?'

'It's the only place where gays can meet in safety in this part of London. I lost my partner a couple of months ago and I get comfort from the casual contact with other men like myself. Unlike Dick though, I only go to James place meet up for a one-to-one relationship. Dick tried it on me once.'

Suddenly Doug started to piece the picture together. James was attempting to relate to him. Did he trust him? Should he make his exit now, or should he stay to learn more? His working relationship was at an end with Dick that was for sure. What was he going to do now?

'Am I your current one to one relationship then?' Doug suddenly asked.

James leaned forward in his chair. He smiled.

'To tell you the truth since I lost my partner, I have not found anyone that I wanted to have a one- to-one with, that is until last night.'

Doug slumped back in his chair spilling his water across his lap.

'Shit, I'm sorry.' Doug said, standing up quickly to avoid the water spilling onto his chair.

James dashed out of the room and returned with a cloth in his hand. The two stared at each other for a second. Doug thought James was going to make the most of the situation by wiping him dry, but instead James handed the cloth to him.

'Don't worry about the chair its only water. Dry your trousers off first.'

If James was going to make any advance, then he had just had the opportunity to do so. Doug wiped his trousers down as James looked on. James then asked if he was comfortable enough in still wearing them or if he wanted to borrow another pair of his. Doug declined the offer. Now his mind was in overdrive as he had a feeling that he had just got himself out of one situation and was about to find himself in another. He stood uncomfortably in his soaked trousers and still holding the towel in his hand. The words of James *'until last night'* still were echoing in his head.

'Look. I think I should be getting back to my lodgings,' Doug suddenly said, handing James the towel back.

'You don't have to go. If you do, can we meet up again?' James said, taking hold of the towel.

The reality of the situation suddenly hit Doug. He could not get into his lodgings at this early hour of the morning. There was no way he could go back and work for Dick again, and he had not yet worked out what James intentions were so far. He had been tempted to come to London in the hope that he could rekindle his feelings for Dick. His head was in turmoil.

'Look old fellow. Why don't you stay here and get some sleep in? You can sleep on the couch in here. I guess you know by now that I find you attractive, but I'm not like Dick and his crowd. You will be quite safe here with me. I'll get you some blankets.'

Doug stood frozen to the floor as he watched James leaving the room. If he was to escape from the situation he was in, now was his chance. There was something about James though that made him stay. He seemed different. He was a rich gay gentleman searching for a companion. Why had James chosen him? There was something about James that attracted him. Too late now though, James had returned carrying his blankets.

'There you are. Make yourself comfortable,' James said as he started spreading the blankets over the couch.

Doug stood there not quite knowing what to do. To his surprise James started to leave the room again without turning to wait for him to undress as he thought he might have done. As he reached the door, James turned, looked back, and smiled for a second.

'Sleep well.'

Trying to sleep with the dawn breaking and in strange surroundings did not go well for him. It was as if he had only just closed his eyes before he was being gently spoken to. He could feel the warm breath and a soft voice in his ear, and then the gentlest of kisses that made him open his eyes.

'I've made you a cup of tea.'

Doug turned over and looked up at James. He stood there wrapped in his white towelling robe, looking freshly handsome. They exchanged looks as if testing each other out.

'I'll leave your tea here on the side of the couch. It's nearly ten o'clock. Don't worry I'm in no rush to go anywhere. Take your time.'

Doug eased his stiff body into a sitting position and reached out for his tea. He smiled at James as he sat there in his robe looking so cool and relaxed. Why was he mixed up with Roger? Why had he taken the trouble to get him out of the situation?

'What will you do now about work? James suddenly asked.

'I'm not going back there. As soon as I can get into my room I'll collect my things and head back home and start again I guess. I don't think London is right for me,' Doug replied.

'Now hold on,' James said. ' Don't be so hasty. I've been in this situation before. If you can hang on a while, I will introduce you so some of my friends I have met the same way as meeting you.'

Doug looked puzzled and drank his tea up in almost one gulp. He sat there waiting for James to say more. He watched as James walked around the room. He cut a fine figure.

'Look Doug. You might like to consider something. You see, I run a male escort agency.'

'A what?'

'A male escort agency. The rich businessmen pay handsomely to have a young man to take to social events.'

'I'm not going to be a male prostitute for you or anyone,' Doug said, making to get out of bed as he spoke, then remembered that he was not wearing anything under his blankets.

James came over to him and sat down on the side of the couch.

'I think you have it wrong. Just wait until you meet the others, then decide. It's easy work and the pay is good. You never have to give yourself to the person that books you,' James said, looking into Doug's nervous flustered face. 'You can live here with me. I'd like that,' he said, leaning forward and reaching out to touch Doug's face gently and bringing their heads together searching for a kiss. 'Come on relax, you have had a bad experience back with Dick, but I'm not like that, else why should I bother to have rescued you?'

As their lips touched, he thought on the question. There was something about James that made him respond to his approach. For a while they kissed, and he searched for comfort in the arms of James.

CHAPTER 13

—⟶·ᴖᴖ·ᴏᴏ·ᴇ·ᴏ·ᴇᴏ·ᴇ·ᴏ·ᴏ·ᴖᴖ·⟵—

Bryan was trying to pass time by tending the front garden for his mother. The sun beat down on his body as he clipped away with the shears at the hedge. He could feel his mother watching him from inside the cottage. He was working away just like his father had done a few years back. Life played funny tricks on the destiny and direction of people's lives. He was deep in thought about Tom when he heard the sound of the rickety front garden gate being opened. He turned to see the Post Lady struggling with the gate.

'Morning. Have a couple of letters here for you Bryan.'

For a moment Bryan stood there not quite knowing what to do. Letters were a rarity. He hurried across the lawn to take hold of the letters, thanked her, and stood excitedly looking at the letters in his hand. One was stamped London and the other was marked Norfolk. His heart raced at the thought of the contents. He was tempted to open and read them there and then but he slipped them into his back pocket and made for the cottage. His mother was in the kitchen so she would not have seen the post lady handing him the letters. She turned on hearing him enter.

'Hello dear. Have you finished the hedge? You look very hot,' she said.

'It is hot out there. I'm going to cool down with some cold water upstairs.'

'Would you like a tea?'

'No thanks.'

He hurried upstairs and made extra noises in the bathroom so as his mother could hear him. Why should he feel so guilty about getting letters from Tom and Doug? He entered his bedroom and stretch himself out on his bed. Which of the two letters should he read first? He waved them in his hand like a fan as he made his choice. His hand began to shake a little as he fumbled to open the letter from Doug first. He thought he would get this one read first so that he could take his time in reading Tom's letter. His fingers made a mess of the envelope as he opened it. He read the letter quickly as it contained loads of details as to what had happened in Doug's life since going to London. Although he was anxious to read Tom's letter he just had to go over Doug's in more detail. What he was reading was a confusing account of events. He read the last page again so that he could clear his mind as to Doug's situation. He lay back on the bed and stared at the letter. How on earth could such a nice bloke get himself involved in a gay scene like Doug had? And what was more, it seemed as if he was going to stay in London and get himself deeper into the scene. He lay there for a while trying to understand what he had just read. His heart began to beat faster as he attempted to open the letter from Tom. This was the one he really wanted to read.

My Dearest Bryan,

I want to say so much in this letter, but I am not good at writing. When I left you I realised that I had made a mess of my visit. You see, I think I'm gay but I'm not sure, that is the reason I did not return your love. I cried as I sat on the train going home as I then realised that I wanted to make love to you, but it was too late then. I can't write any more words that could explain my feelings now.

My parents are going away for a month at the end of next week, that's the 29th. I hope you can come up and stay with me for a while. Unless I have a phone call from you on Wednesday evening I trust you will find your way up here. I have looked up the times of the train you can catch [see note for times and directions enclosed]

Can't wait to hold you in my arms again [God, did I write that?]

Much Love,
Tom x

He read the letter again and again as he lay there on his bed with a smile across his face and glancing at the letter still in his hand. To think, he was going to spend a couple of weeks with Tom. But how was his mother going to understand? Should he tell her about his love for Tom? Best not.

His mind ran riot as he fantasised being in Norfolk with Tom with the freedom of being alone with him. What was it going to be like making love to him? Supposing they failed to make love together? He knew he was going to feel nervous when it came to the final act. But then married couples must go through the same emotions when they first meet. He loved Tom, he knew that, and so it was only natural that he should feel nervous. He felt a funny sensation run through the whole of his body at the thought of having Tom in his arms. It was going to be a long week ahead of him.

As he sat at the kitchen table having tea that afternoon, he suddenly felt a hot flush come over him as he tried to pluck up courage to tell his mother of the coming trip away from home. There was a feeling of guilt raged through his body as he realised that she was going to be left alone once again.

To his surprise when the words came out of his dry mouth, his mother only smiled and continued to busy herself in getting tea.

'It will do you good to get away for a change of scenery,' she said. 'I expect his parents will find it strange having another man around their house.'

'They are going to be on holiday, Tom tells me. They haven't had a holiday in years.' As he spoke he nearly plucked up courage to tell her about his feelings for Tom.

He began counting the days till he met up with Tom. He had walked to the railway station a couple of times to check on the times of trains to Norfolk. His mother had told him off a few times about his restlessness and how he was getting on her nerves a little. A statement she wished she had never made. The evening before his departure they both became on edge. He had packed his case once, then unpacked and removed a few clothes to make it lighter. That night he drifted in and out of sleep with excitement, and he was glad when the morning daylight started to appear through his bedroom window. His mother had been troubled with lack of sleep too and had made an early start on her housework. The parting was a little emotional. He looked back and waved as he closed the front garden gate. The long walk down the lane to the station eased his tensions for him. His body tingled with excitement as he paid for his ticket and walked onto the platform to wait for the arrival of his train. He knew he was going to have to change trains once, so he could not afford to sleep. He tried hard to read his book, but he could not concentrate long enough. He watched the beautiful countryside rolling past his window and contented himself in just staring out into space. Having changed trains with little delay, he once again settled down for the rest of the journey. His mind suddenly returned to France and the bleak countryside he had become used to. He smiled as he watched the green of the trees and hedgerow flash past him. How he had missed England during the war. Checking his watch he worked out that within the hour he would be with Tom again. His heart seemed to be beating faster at the thought of what he was getting himself into. Once again he began to challenge his sexuality and he continued deep in thought until he suddenly realised the train was slowing down. He opened the window and looked out. Yes, he could see the station ahead.

His heart missed a beat with excitement. He reached up for his case up in the rack above his head and almost dropped it in his excited state. There was a cloud of smoke and steam as the train slowed down to a halt along the platform. He searched through the smoke in search of Tom. As the smoke cleared he could see a lone figure standing at the other end of the platform. He waved as he hurried towards the figure. Yes, it was Tom, and he waved back. They drew nearer. Now they were standing close to each other face to face. Not a word was spoken at first. Their eyes searched each others. It was a magical sensation as the chemistry radiated between them. They both knew they were in love. They were desperate to kiss and hold each other in their arms. Just for the moment though they were content to settle for the wash of emotional love and chemistry between them, a rare moment in life. What was it about Tom's face that made him so perfect? Was it his eyes, so deeply set and the deep brown mystery they created? He looked at his high cheekbones and the way his sculptured mouth gave way to a smile and the flash of whiter than white teeth his grin exposed. Tom was surely one of the most perfect men he had observed since his interest in his own sex.

'Oh God, it's so nice in seeing you again, 'Tom said, having surveyed Bryan as he had been surveyed. He placed his hand on Bryan's shoulder and gave it a shrug, so firm, so warm.

'God, how I've missed you,' Bryan replied.

'How was your journey?'

'Long, but well worth it now I'm here.'

'Come on. Let's get away from this place. I can't wait to show you our home. You'll love it.'

'I hope I've got my own personal room,' Bryan laughed nervously.

Tom laughed as he gave a gentle shove of his hand on Bryan's back. They walked out into the station forecourt. Tom gave a sigh, flung his arms wide as he looked for the bus.

'I think we have just missed the bus. Guess we have a long walk ahead of us,' Tom announced.

'I'm not bothered. I've been sitting far too long,' Bryan replied.

They took turns in carrying the suitcase and there was little conversation between them, they were deep in their own thoughts. Bryan was beginning to feel a little tense as reality was setting in. Once out of the town and finding themselves walking alone down the country lanes, Bryan reached out to take hold of Tom's hand and found it warm with sweat like his own. He found it frustrating in having to hide his feelings for Tom from the rest of the world. To him it was natural in wanting to relate to Tom. His fear now was if Tom wanted to commit himself to him. Commit. This was a difficult word to digest. He was about to venture into a relationship which not many people could understand. His thoughts switched to the letter he had received from Doug. How sad was that for a young man get himself involved in some kind of group sex. Then he smiled at his own thoughts.

How lucky he was to have found Tom. He didn't have to share him with anyone. He gave Tom's hand a squeeze. Tom looked round at him and smiled.

'We are nearly there now. Look, that's my parents house up there, just around the bend,' Tom said.

Bryan looked up above the hedgerow where he caught sight of the chimneys and roof top of what looked like a large house.

'Is this where you live? Christ, what a massive place.'

Tom held open the front gate set in a brick archway and ushered Bryan through. As they reached the steps leading to the front door, Tom fumbled for the front door key. Once the door was opened, Bryan entered and stood in the hallway looking up at the size of the place. How small his own cottage must have seemed to Tom.

'Christ, what a house.'

'Like it?' Tom smiled.

'I think I could manage living here,' Bryan replied.

Tom placed the suitcase down that he had been carrying for the last mile and rubbed his arm. They stood there in silence for a while before Tom made the first move. He reached out and put his arms around Bryan pulling him towards him. They embraced. Bryan felt the warmth of Tom's breath against the side of his face. Then slowly their heads turned and their lips caressed gently at first.

'God how I have wanted to do this with you,' Tom said. 'I made a mess of things when I visited you, and I promise I won't do that again. Their mouths and tongues searched in a feverish frenzy as they showed their love for each other. Tom pulled away for a moment to gasp for breath. He searched into Bryan's eyes and he was reassured of the returned love. Tom kissed him gently on the lips again and released his arms from around him. They smiled at each other.

'Let me show you your room.'

Bryan was a little taken aback by the inference that he we going to have his own room and that they were not sharing a bed. The landing was long having several doors along it.

'Here we are, your room. Hope you like it,' Tom said opening the door for Bryan to enter. The room was large and quite airy. The first thing that Bryan focused on was the size of the double bed. He turned to Tom who was standing there smiling.

'So where is your room then?' Bryan asked.

'You are standing in it,' Tom replied.

'You sod.'

'You didn't think I was going to make a mess of your visit like I did when I visited you, did you?'

Bryan laughed as he flung himself onto the bed and bounce himself around. Tom watched him and was tempted to join him, but something held him back. They remained silent and unsure as to how they should deal with their first moments together. Bryan sat up on the edge of the bed. He smiled as he realised that Tom was standing there with his hands deep inside his trouser pockets. He knew what his problem was as he was beginning to feel a stirring between thighs as well. Tom looked coy and embarrassed standing there. Bryan opened his arms out wide, and this was just the move Tom was waiting for. They fell into each other's arms and rolled around on the bed with hands searching each other's bodies in a frantic fever. Moments passed and they kissed as if there was no tomorrow. Soon there were moves from Bryan to start removing Tom's clothes, but Tom seemed to want to say something. Their lips parted, and Tom drew in a deep breath as he struggled to sit up on the bed. Bryan had a deep frown on his forehead. He was concerned that Tom was going to react in the same way as he had at the cottage.

'Bryan, my lover, I'd like to take it easy. I want it to be so right when we…you know.'

'I'm sorry. I just want to have your love. But, you are right. I think we should get out of this bedroom it's giving me ideas,' Bryan said, looking a little sheepish.

'Let me show you the rest of the house.'

'Fine, lead the way.'

Bryan was amazed at the size of the house. But the gardens were even more amazing. They set themselves down in deck chairs under the shade of the silver birch trees in the centre of the lawns.

There conversation soon turned to their past lives. They both found that they were virgins and that this was to be their first experience of making love with another man.

'Does that scare you like it scares me?' Tom asked.

Bryan stretched out his hand in search of Tom's hand. He thought on the question for a second.

'I'm not sure that sacred is the word. I'm just excited. Yes, I think I'll be shit scared that I get it right if we do it tonight,' Bryan said.

'Me too,' Tom replied, but I think we should just let it happen as it happens, if you know what I mean. There are so many things that worry me though.'

'Such as what?'

'Well, I don't feel gay, yet I want to have you,' Tom said. I have no experience with women apart from the odd fumble at a party. It didn't do anything for me. I tried it a couple of times when I was about sixteen, but no change in my feelings. Women don't excite me sexually.'

'And I do then?' Bryan said, smiling as he spoke

'Too bloody true you do. You wait till later and I'll prove that to you.'

They laughed together. For now they were breaking the ice between them. It was the first move to acceptance to the fact that they were gay.

'What about you then?' Tom asked.

Bryan thought this was the time to tell of his brief encounter with Doug. Tom listened with a frown on his face.

'Do you think you will go back home to Doug then?'

'Shit no.'

'How can you be so sure about that?'

Bryan then told him the whole story and the letter he had received from Doug.

'It sounds as if he has made a right fuck-up of his life then.'

'You could say that. I just could not get involved in a sex scene or have sex with just anyone like that. I would feel I was having sex just for the sake of it. I just want a loving relationship.'

There was a silence and calm that came over them as they sat there in the garden.

After having sat down to a meal and sharing a couple of beers, they spent the rest of the evening sitting around a log fire in the lounge. Tom was the first to make the first move by spreading himself out in front of the fire and making himself comfortable with a few cushions around him. He gestured for Bryan to join him. He needed little persuasion. As the fire sparked and sputtered in the hearth, the low light added to their sexual heightening. They kissed and caressed until it became impossible to put off the temptation of having sex together any longer. Slowly they remove each others clothing until they lay there letting the firelight cast golden patterns across their naked bodies exposing themselves to each other. It was as if all inhibitions were removed from the room.

Bryan's hands explored Tom's body in slow sensuous teasing tests. His fingers drifted across Tom's soft but firm lips. Tom kissed the fingers as if to add permission to explore into more depths.

Bryan ran his fingers down along Tom's neck and down onto his chest. He felt Tom give a little shudder at his tender touches. As Bryan found and began to tease his nipples and raise them to a firmness. Tom moaned his approval and his body arched for more. It was a marvellous new experience they were enjoying together. Tom placed his hand over Bryan's, and in return asked if he could do the same for him. Once again there was no resistance from his lover at his side. Bryan gave a cry of joy as he felt Tom kiss and tease his nipple. Like all men, they at times gained enjoyment from teasing their own nipples during self pleasure times in secret, but to have another doing this for him was beyond his wildest imagination. They both remained content in giving pleasure in this way to each other, and there was no attempt to take their love making any further at that stage. The fire was roasting them to a point were they lay there with perspiration which all added to the sensuous mood they were experiencing. Tom whispered that he thought it would be a good idea to take a bath together. Bryan lay there in a dream, and nodded his approval. As Tom turned over to stand up, Bryan reached out to take hold of the erection confronting him. They laughed a Tom teased him a little by doing a little jig in front of the fire letting his erect penis sway.

The bath was hot and inviting as they both climbed in. The water line rose high as they sank their bodies under the water with hands searching to take hold of their erections. They played and soaped each other, laughing and exchanging kisses until the water began to cool. They dried each other as they stood there now completely uninhibited in their nakedness, yet both feeling unsure of what was expected of each other. The bedclothes were pulled back and then over them as they slid between the sheets and their naked bodies entwined with excitement. They kissed and embraced with a feverish urgency with hands searching for pleasure points to be enjoyed. A sigh ensured the other that the spot had been found and a desire to have this explored more. Their erections were throbbing as never before. And like most first time lovers the excitement proved to be too much to be ignored for long. Tom was the first to make the move that was to bring union and an end to virginity. In his excitement he entered Bryan without too much foreplay. They both gasped aloud as they experienced the sensations they had only dream of, but it was all over in a flash as Tom had only thrust himself a few times before he cried out his failure to stay the pace. He fell at Bryan's side and they lay there in silence for a while.

'Fuck,' Tom eventually cried out aloud as he lay there trying to stimulate himself back into life.

Bryan reached out his arm to cradle him and comfort him in his embarrassment.

'Come on. Don't worry about it. We have two weeks to practice and make perfect,' Bryan said.

Tom curled up into Bryan's arms with his hand placed across Bryan's chest only to feel the thumping of Bryan's heart beating fast. They lay there in the soft light of the bedside lamp not wanting to speak about the situation. Tom was questioning himself about the way he had fouled up the evening. How could he have been so stupid in wanting to be the aggressor out of the two? If only he had given himself time to have some foreplay instead of acting like an excited schoolboy who had just had his first erection. He raised his head to find Bryan laying there with his eyes shut.

'Do you want to try again?' Tom asked him.

'Lets just enjoy being with each other. I just love the feel of your body.'

Midnight arrived and they had just let their hands and lips explore each other. Tom had thought that he could try again before the night slipped by, but somehow his nerve had let him down. He thought that Bryan had drifted off to sleep. Oh God, how frustrated he must be he thought. He turned over onto his side and settled his pillow ready for sleep. He felt Bryan turn towards him and his arms wrap across his chest and pulling him closer. His body shuddered at the feel of Bryan's erection in the small of his back. He murmured his approval as he then felt Bryan's hand searching and teasing for entrance. Oh how great that felt. Without even a doubt of failure, Bryan entered and began a gentle movement as Tom took him in with small thrusts at first. The feeling was making him dizzy, and he bit his lip at the pressure he was feeling. There was no pain as he had thought there might be, and the sensation was like he had never known in his life before. They rocked together as Bryan's rhythm started to increase. Soon they were moving in harmony together and kept up the pace until there was that eruptive feeling that seemed to rage through their bodies and finding themselves in a state of almost loosing consciousness.

'Oh shit that was great,' Tom cried out, not wanting it to end.

'We made love. Shit, we made love together,' Bryan called aloud, as he withdrew himself and lay at Tom's side.

They pulled the bedclothes high up over their heads and snuggled down in each other's arms.

'I love you so much. Do you think we are wrong in loving each other like this?' Tom asked.

'I don't know, and I really don't care.'

'Do you think married couples enjoy their sex life like we do?' Tom asked, running his hand across Bryan's chest then down to his pubic area where he just fumbled his fingers amongst the thick bush of hair. Does a woman really know how and where to touch a man?'

'Oh listen to mister experience,' Bryan laughed.

'No. I'm serious. How can a woman really know what a man likes?'

'I don't think they could ever know. I can't ever think of my parents making love like us, Bryan said. 'But then, I never really gave it much thought. 'They must have done it three times at least as I have two sisters.'

They laughed under the bedclothes. Somehow they both felt secure down there.

Sleep eventually overcame the two of them, and they slept through the rest of the night in each other's arms. Next morning Bryan was aware that Tom was not at his side. He turned over and looked towards the window. Tom was sitting on the window ledge with the new morning sunshine sculpturing his nakedness in beautiful truth. He remained still and without making a sound as he drank in the youthful frame of his lover. Tom was deep in thought, then he suddenly aware that he was being observed. He smiled and held out his hand for Bryan to join him. He watched as Bryan pulled back the bedclothes and sat for a moment on the edge of the bed rubbing his hands through his tussled hair. They embraced as they stared out into the gardens below.

'Good morning,' Tom smiled.

'Any regrets?' Bryan asked.

'I wish that I could have stayed long enough to make you happy.'

Bryan gave him s a reassuring hug.

CHAPTER 14

─wwᴏᴏᴇᴛᴏᴏᴛᴇᴏᴏww─

They spent the first of their two week break together freely roaming around the house and gardens naked. They did dress for dinner just for the fun of removing each other's clothes during the evening around the log fire in the lounge. They were deliriously happy and in love. It was the Wednesday night of the second week when as they were relaxing reading in bed from the same book together when Tom heard a noise from downstairs. He sat there ridged as he listened to the sound of footsteps coming upstairs. The two looked at each other in fear of what was going on out on the landing. They heard a door open and close again from along the landing. Tom put a finger up to Bryan's lips to silence him. He was sweating. Leaping out of bed, he grabbed his robe and slipped into it. Bryan lay there only able to watch as Tom opened the door and disappeared out onto the landing. He could hear voices, but couldn't make out what was being said. It seemed ages before Tom returned. He looked flushed and nervous as he spoke.

'They are back. Shit. They have come home early,' Tom whispered.

'Your parents are home?' Bryan whispered back.

'Yes. My mum was taken ill, so they cut short their holiday. Shit.'

They both stared at each other not quite knowing what to do. Bryan made to get out of bed, but Tom ushered him back under the covers.

'What are we going to do?' Bryan asked.

Tom removed his dressing gown and pulled back the covers and climbed back into bed, much to Bryan's surprise. They both sat there frozen to the mattress. Neither spoke for a while.

'I asked you what we were going to do,' Bryan said. 'Should I creep out of the house tonight?'

'No. I think this is the time to break the news about me being gay to my parents.'

Bryan felt quite ill at the thought of being around when Tom announce the situation to them.

'You aren't going to do that tonight, are you?' Bryan asked nervously.

'No, I couldn't face that tonight, plus the fact that mum's not too good. Best try and get some sleep in. God, that's put an end to our love in.'

'I couldn't sleep now. I think I should leave,' Bryan said.

'Please don't,' Tom pleaded.

'I think you might be able to put off telling them if I wasn't around.'

'Look. Do you love me?' Tom asked.

'You know I do.'

'Well then stay. If I am to tell my parents the truth, then they might as well know who you are.'

Bryan lay back in bed and gave the situation some thought. Tom lay down at his side and kissed him gently on the lips. They pulled the bedclothes up over them and settled down to try a get some sleep in before the balloon went up in the morning. They both tossed and turned in bed all night.

They were awakened by a loud knocking on the bedroom door.

'Tea,' a voice could be heard from the other side of the door, then the door handle turned and there stood Tom's father in his dressing gown holding a cup of tea in his hand.

Tom sat erect upright in bed, and Bryan ducked down deeper under the covers.

'What the hell is going on?' Tom's father demanded. 'Have you a woman in bed with you? Good Lord. I never thought you would do this behind our backs.'

There was a deadly silence between the three of them. Bryan was shivering now, and Tom was trying to think of something to say. Words failed him.

'I'll take your tea back downstairs. You can explain yourself when to choose to join us downstairs with your…eh…friend.'

Bryan heard the door slam closed and appeared up out of the covers. Tom had his fist in his mouth.

'Are you going downstairs?' Bryan asked.

'I don't think I have an option. They have to know sometime. I just have to face the music.'

'I'm with you then,' Bryan spluttered.

Once washed and shaved, they both headed downstairs. Bryan's legs had lost all sense of feeling now as he stood behind Tom at the kitchen door. Tom turned around and gave him a brief kiss on his cheek. His face looked white with fear. They could hear raised voices coming from the other side of the door. They tried to listen with their ears against the door. Suddenly the door open sharply and they came face to face with Tom's father. He stared at Bryan as if he had seen a ghost.

'Who the hell are you?'

Tom cleared his voice, but words did not come easy.

'Dad, this is my friend Bryan.'

There was a deadly hush as the three of them exchanged looks. Bryan offered his hand, but he knew this was a stupid gesture. Tom's father was in no mood to shake hands with him.

'Bryan and I were in the army together. We were in the trenches. He got injured too.'

'So why didn't you put your friend in one of the spare bedrooms?' Tom's father boomed out.

'Well dad, I guess you will have to know sooner than later, Bryan is more than a friend.'

'What are you trying to tell me?'

Tom cleared his throat. He looked over the shoulder of his father to see the expression on his mothers face. She was sitting at the kitchen table with her head in her hands.

'I'm gay dad. Sorry, but I have to tell you that I'm gay.'

'Rubbish. You can't go to war being a gay. You have to be a real man to be a soldier. You must have had more than just a leg injury out there. It must have affected your head. You are not gay.'

'I'm in love with Bryan.

'You have the nerve to bring this...this person into our home and sleep with him. What the hell are you telling me my *man*...I take that word back...'

'I'm telling you dad that I am gay...I'm sorry, I didn't want to be, but I am.

Bryan went to say something, but his voice had gone. Tom's father saw his attempt to speak.

'And you can shut up.'

Bryan shook his head and felt quite helpless.

'Don't talk like that to Bryan,' Tom responded.

'I'll talk as I please. This is my house if I may remind you. Your friend is not welcome here.'

'If Bryan is not welcome, them neither am I,' Tom said, his voice now very shaky and weak.

Father and son stood staring at each other for a moment before he closed the door in their faces.

Tom shrugged his shoulders, turned and fell into Bryan's arms for reassurance. They hugged each other for a moment, and then the door opened again. It was Tom's mother. She looked tired and pale as she closed the door behind her and reached out to Tom.

'Darling, don't listen to your father, he doesn't mean what he said.'

'Mum, it's alright; it must have come as a shock to him. Oh, this is Bryan.'

His mother half smiled, but made no attempt to speak to him.

'What will you do now?'

'I have to leave home for a while. I just hope that dad is able to forgive me,' Tom said.

He turned and cuddled his mother for a moment, and then he headed upstairs again to pack some things in a suitcase. Bryan stood at his side not quite knowing what to do or say. He felt so sorry for Tom, but then he also felt sorry for his parents. It was not Tom's choice that he was born gay, but neither was it his parent fault. He felt sad that his parents could not find room in their hearts to accept the situation and let love overcome everything. Bryan then began to think of how his mother and his sisters were going to react, for now he had no alternative but to return home and take Tom with him. Oh my God that was quite a thought. Supposing his mother reacted in the same way. What the hell would they both do with their lives? Society also rejected men's love for each other.

As they both left the house with their suitcases, Tom's mother clung to his arm pleading with him not to think too badly of his father. Where are you going to stay?' she asked.

'I'll take him to my home,' Bryan said.

'I hope your parents accept you both.'

Bryan gave a half smile and nodded in the hope that this helped to reassure her that Tom would be fine and not all was lost. Tom and his mother kissed and hugged one more time. Tom's mother then turned to Bryan. There were no signs that she wanted to even shake his hand, but she spoke.

'You take good care of Tom. I can't understand either of you, but if anything happens to him, don't think that you could ever hide from his father and myself.'

As the two walked away from the house and back down the lanes towards the station, they remained silent. Bryan had not even thought as to where they were going, and Tom assumed that Bryan was taking him back to Cambridge. They just kept walking in silence. There world had been shattered around them. They had an hour to wait before the train was due, so they had plenty of time to talk about the next move.

'Do you know what you are doing in taking me home to your mum?' Tom asked.

'No. But if you think I'm going to lose you now, you have read me wrong. We could live anywhere we choose. But my home is the first place to try.'

'Will your mother understand us?'

'I have no idea.'

They were glad to see the train approaching the station. They searched for an empty carriage and settled down for the journey into the unknown.

CHAPTER 15

—⁓·∾ᴏⱻᴐᴏᴇ⌇ᴐ·∿—

With his mother not having a phone in the cottage, there was no way Bryan could let her know that he was arriving home with Tom. As they approached the cottage carrying their suitcases, there was a nervous tension running between them. They had gone over the situation they were in a few times, but they had no set plan in mind. If Bryan was to be rejected by his mother, then they would have to find a B&B for the night. But then what? They were both feeling dejected and tired from their journey. They stood at the front gate of the cottage for a while not wanting to have to face what they feared. Bryan saw movements in the curtains, there was no going back. As they approached the front door it opened. His mother greeted him with open arms.

'Darling how lovely to see you. Back so soon, and look who you have brought with you,' she smiled. 'Come in you both look exhausted.'

Bryan embraced his mother and made his way down the hall into the kitchen. As Tom eased himself past Bryan's mum, she squeezed his arm and smiled at him.

'Wish you were on the phone mum,' Bryan said, 'I could have phoned you.'

'Yes, then I could have told you that your sister is due to arrive later today.'

Bryan froze on the spot on hearing this. His mind raced away as he would have to tell her as well as his mother. Christ, what a mess.

'Are they both coming?' Bryan asked.

'Just Tina, she is coming up by car. Her friend is in Cambridge on business and is dropping her off.

It's only for an overnight visit as her friend has to return back home.'

Tom glanced at Bryan. He didn't know what to read into Bryan's expression. Fear came to mind.

'Sit down both of you. Would you like some tea?'

They both sat down at the kitchen table watching his mother busy herself. How on earth was he going to tell his mother about Tom and himself? There was no way he could just blurt it out, but how else was there. As his mother sat down with them and poured the tea into the mugs, she eyed the two of them as if she knew something that they didn't. Surely she hadn't guessed that he was gay? He took hold of his mug of tea and sipped at the hot brew.

'Why are you home so early?'

Bryan cleared his throat. He saw Tom slide down in his chair as he was about start talking.

'It's a long story mum, and I'm not sure that you will like hearing it.'

'For goodness sake, I don't think much could shock me now at my age. Get on with it.'

He started by telling his mother how they both used to crouch together in the trenches as the shelling continued day and night sometimes. His mother's face showed emotions as she listened.

'We became more than friends mum.'

'Go on.'

'Well when I came home I missed Tom so much, that's why I invited him down to stay.'

His mother looked across the table at Tom. His face was white with fear.

'Do you know what I am trying to tell you mum?'

There was a long silence as the three of them sipped at their tea. Bryan tried to continue, but his mother reached out her hand towards him. He took hold of it, and she squeezed it tightly.

'My darling Bryan,' she said, I don't confess to know why or how you get comfort from another man like Tom, but I am only glad that you came home safely from that dreadful war. I was speaking to Mrs Vine. I think you know that Doug is…well you know…the same as you two.'

'How long have you known about me then?'

'I didn't really want to believe it, but I watched you two when you were together. I tell you, I prefer that it be Tom than her son Doug.

163

Mrs Vine told me that Doug liked you a lot…but I have never been sure about him, glad he went to London.'

Bryan felt the need to comfort his mother. He got up from the table and threw his arms around her. Tom could only look on trying to stifle a tear back at the scene.

'Mum. I'm so sorry about this having to come out like this. But there was no other way of telling you. Are you upset?'

'Upset. No. Disappointed is the word. But as I have said, at least you are home safe and well. Now are you going to tell me why you are home early from Tom's parent's house?'

Tom gave a loud cough. Bryan's mother held out her hand across the table. Tom reached across and took hold of hers. He then went on to tell her about his parents reactions and how he was asked to leave the house. He didn't tell her how they had been found in bed by his father.

'I'm sure, given time they will forgive you. After all you are their son.'

They adjourned to the garden where they talked about the future. Bryan's mother was prepared for Tom to stay with them for a while as long as he could pay her some money to help feed him. Tom told her that he was quite well off having been left monies by his Grandmother. Then Bryan approached the subject of them sharing a room.

'You have no choice Tina arrives. I'm not having her sleeping down here on a couch,' she smiled.

'Talking of Tina, what time will she arrive?'

'She said about seven o'clock.'

'Well I think Tom and I would like to unpack our things mum,' Bryan said, winking at Tom.

They left mum in the garden then hurried upstairs and collapsed on the bed in Bryan's room.

'God, your mother is a dream. How could she have known all the time? Were we that obvious when I stayed? What do you think your sister will say when she arrives?'

Bryan flung his arms around him and gave a snigger of a laugh. He suddenly felt nervous at the thought of having to face his sister. He wondered if she had detected his gayness earlier.

'I don't know. All I am pleased about is that my mum has taken it so well.'

They unpacked their cases and laughed as they started to share the drawer space in the wardrobe and chest of drawers. Next towels were hung over the towel rails in the bathroom and their tooth brushes stood side by side in a glass on the ledge under the mirror. These were only simple things, but it brought tender feelings of being together as one for the first time in their lives. They were two men just about to experience a tender bonding that they were not sure was natural to men of their stature. They had been through a war and hardship together. They had know what it was like to have fired bullets across the barren land that divided them from the enemy trenches knowing that they might have killed a life or two in the process. And now they were home in England again trying to piece their lives together, so was it their fault that they were drawn together like this?

All these strange questions raced through both their heads and there were moments of silence between them as they wrestled with their emotions. They sat on the bed again and exchanged their inner thoughts and emotions as if they were searching for a meaning to life. After a while, they rejoined Bryan's mother in the garden, still confused about their sexuality. His mother had offered to make a pot of tea, leaving them both sitting in deckchairs deep in thought once again. Tom was feeling nervous as he recalled his failure to perform that first night in his own bed back home. What if he failed again? What would this mean about his relationship with Bryan for he knew that he wanted to be taken in the same way as he had been? He consoled himself with the thought that he had read somewhere that heterosexual males quite often experienced the same problems at times. He lay there and studied Bryan as he rested his head against the back of his deckchair. He really was quite gorgeous looking. How lucky he was to have found him out there in France. His thoughts were broken by the sound of a car engine coming from down the lane towards the cottage. Bryan sat up suddenly and there was a shout from his mother from the kitchen. Tina had arrived. Tom struggled to collect himself as he stood up and make his exit from the family reunion. Bryan made to grab his arm as he was passing him.

'Don't dash off. I'd like to introduce you to my sister.'

Tom stopped in his tracks and realised that he was not facing up to the situation. He had just sat down again when Tina appeared through the garden gate and approached them. Mother flung her arms around her daughter and hugged the breath out of her. Tina laughed. Bryan stood up and prised his mother away so that he could also greet his sister.

'Come on you two,' he said. 'Make room for me.'

As Tina kissed Bryan, she whispered in his ear to ask to be introduced to his friend. Bryan released his hold on her, and turning he smiled at Tom standing there not quite knowing how to react.

'Tina. This is my very best friend Tom. You remember Tom and I were together in France.'

'I've heard a lot about you Tom,' she said, holding out her hand to greet him.

'Pleased to meet you,' Tom said as they shook hands.

'You never told me that he was so good looking,' Tina teased.

Tom looked embarrassed and put his hands behind his back, then stood at Bryan's side. Bryan, without thinking, went to place his arms around Tom's waist but refrained from doing so. Tina spotted this and smiled at the situation they found themselves in. Mother had stood back watching the body language of all three. She then brushed her apron down and suggested that a cup of tea was called for. Tina followed her mother into the kitchen. Both Tom and Bryan could see the two of them in deep conversation as they busied themselves at the kitchen sink.

'Do you think your mother is telling Tina about us?' Tom asked.

'You can bet on that. She really is an angel. She would do that to make it easier for both Tina and myself. She knows that I would fuck it up if I had to tell Tina myself.'

They both sat there in the garden feeling nervous and waiting for a call from mum to join them with the tea, or for Tina to join them alone. The time seemed to drag. Surely Tina and mum could not be discussing the situation still. The back door suddenly opened. Bryan dared to look around to see Tina approaching. Tom slid down into his deckchair even deeper. Tina sat down by Bryan's chair and curled her legs up under her. She rested her arms on his knees and stared up into his face.

'Well, well. Mum has told me all about you two. I hope you both know what you are doing. Society does not treat people like you very well. There's work to consider. Not many firms would employ you. I just can't understand you Bryan. What the hell happened to my brother?'

There was a strange silence between the three of them and nervous glances exchanged. Tom went to speak, but Tina shot a stern look in his direction.

'I just don't know how two men can enjoy sex together like that,' Tina said.

'Like what?' Bryan retorted.

'Well… you know.'

'No. I don't know.'

'Well I'm sure you just don't hold hands all the time,' Tina said, her voice getting louder.

'It's not all about sex,' Tom interrupted.

'You just keep out of this. This is my brother I'm talking to.'

'Don't be so bloody rude Tina.'

'Sorry. But someone has to say something.'

'Do they? How bloody interesting.'

'Well if it's not all about sex, tell me what else is it all about?'

'I... sorry... we just prefer being together. We are comfortable with being together.'

Tina gave a long hard look at Tom.

'Comfortable.' I see that's a word for it then. You are comfortable in bed.'

'Oh... do leave off for Christ's sake. I thought you might try to understand,' Bryan said.

Tina turned her back on both of them and strutted her way indoors. Tom stood there with his arms stretched wide. He looked glum.

'Do you think I should leave?' Tom asked.

'What! No way. Come on, let's take a walk.'

They got as far as the meadow where they sat down in the long grass and embraced. It was getting dark before they set out to return to the cottage. As they entered the kitchen they were greeted by silence. Tina and her mother just sat there not quite knowing how to handle the situation.

'Would you like a tea?'

'Thanks mum. We are for bed.'

This statement prompted a glad of satisfaction from Tina. She sat there with a smug look on her face as if to say 'I was right then.' Bryan ignored her attempt to raise the subject of their sexuality again. He kissed his mother and then went to kiss his sister as well. All he managed was to brush her cheek with an attempted kiss. Tom just smiled at mum and then made his way upstairs. Once inside their room they hurriedly undressed and climbed into bed. They caressed each other, but somehow neither attempted to engage in love making. They lay there staring up at the moonlight that streamed in through the window. There was no reason to talk. They were comfortable in each others arms. Neither wanted sleep to arrive. It was nearly midnight when Bryan pulled the blankets off and went to look out of the bedroom window.

'I can't sleep. It's so beautiful out there in the moonlight. How about gong for a swim?'

Tom joined him at the window and their two bodies nestled together. They laughed in silence as they watched their erections spring to life. For a moment they were tempted to engage in love making, but Bryan insisted that they took a swim first. Without dressing and with just towels in their hands they ventured out of the room. The coast was clear as Tina and mother were tucked up in their own beds now. They tiptoed downstairs like two naughty schoolboys skipping class as they slipped out into the night. The meadow grass was wet with due which added to the excitement of the moment. Soon they found themselves running along the tow-path where the waters became deeper. They slid down the banking and started swimming towards the willow tree. They laughed together at their naked freedom. At one point their bodies entwined and they kissed and caressed with excited actions. Bryan was the first to reach the willow tree where he climbed up onto the now smooth trunk and taunted Tom's efforts to join him. Soon they were sitting side by side holding onto each other in an embrace. They watched the stars up there in the clear night's sky.

'It's so peaceful out here. Oh, if only your sister would try and understand,' Tom said.

'Don't worry about her. I know she will soon come around and forgive us.'

'Forgive.'

'Yes. I find it difficult to accept the fact that we are different to the way society would have us be.'

'Do you feel we are wrong?'

'No I don't,' Bryan said.

They sat there in silence for quite a while. Suddenly Bryan held on to Tom's arm and gestured with his finger to his lips to remain silent.

'What's up?' Tom whispered.

'Listen,' Bryan whispered back.

There in the distance they could hear the sound of splashing of water. They peered into the semi darkness. Someone was swimming towards them. A shaft of moonlight highlighted the naked form of Tina swimming towards them. Tom went to lower his nakedness down into the water but he was too late and remained sitting where he was. Tina reached out her hand to be helped up onto the trunk of the tree.

Make way for a small one,' she called out.

Both Bryan and Tom reached down to haul her up alongside them. She sat down between them and flipped her fingers through her wet hair.

'Goodness me I'm not as fit as I used to be,' she panted. Then looking at Tom sitting there with his hands protecting his private area, she placed hand on his shoulder and smiled.

'I have to say I'm sorry about the way I spoke to you this evening. I was quite out of order. Sorry.'

'Don't worry. I'm getting used to being judged before I have a chance to explain things,' Tom replied. I can't help the way I am. And I know how you feel as it's your brother I am in love with.'

'I just don't understand either of you. If I was not spoken for, I think I might try to get to know you better. In fact, I'd be making a pass at you myself. But to find that you are my brother's lover, it came as a shock. I'll never understand.' Tina said.

'Then please try,' replied Tom.

Bryan had just sat there alongside them listening. He felt that it was good to let the two of them talk on the matter. He had smiled at the comment that Tina made about making a pass at Tom. That would have been interesting to see if Tina had not already known about their relationship. The three of them remained silent for a while. It was as if they were waiting for each other to make more observations about the situation. Tina then coughed to clear her throat.

'What's it like to have sex together?' Tina asked.

Tom laughed aloud and looked across to Bryan. He gave a broad smile at the cheek of the question. Tina sat there waiting for a response.

'Fucking great,' Bryan suddenly said.

'There is no need to swear,' Tina replied.

'Well you have a nerve. It's like me asking you what it is like in having sex with James, your husband. Come to think of it, how is it with you two, or has the romance gone out of your lives?'

'I don't think this is getting us anywhere little brother of mine.'

'Oh for Christ sake Tina, there is no way I'm going to talk about my sex life with Tom. I know you don't understand, but I'm really in love with him.'

'Well that's all that matters to me. I'm sorry I don't understand you both…but as long as you are both happy, then that's great for me and mum.'

With that, Tina suddenly kissed Tom on his cheek, then turning, she did the same to Bryan, slid her naked body down under the water and swam away back in the direction of home. Tom and Bryan just sat there in silence watching Tina swimming out of sight and trying to make sense of their conversation with her.

'Sorry about that,' Bryan eventually said. 'She is a strong willed woman.'

'Do you think she meant what she said about making a pass at me?'

'Yes. But I made the first pass. But if you feel you want to go with a woman...then I wont stand in your way.'

Tom laughed aloud and made a lunge at Bryan knocking him off of the tree trunk and into the water. He then slid himself down under the water and took hold of Bryan's leg. They wrestled like two school boys at play. Their heads both appeared on the surface, and they gasped for breath. They embraced, kissed and fondled each other. They were at peace with the world now that their lifestyle had been accepted by Tina and her mother, maybe not as well as they would have liked, but accepted They swam back through the darkness, climbed up the banking and made their way through the meadow and back into the cottage. As they climbed the stairs trying not to make a noise, they suddenly became aware that they were being observed by mum as she returned from the bathroom to her room along the landing. They froze on the top stair holding their breath their hands over their privates.

'Oh, don't be so coy with me. Don't you think I have known all along that you never swam in your costumes in all your life? I think it's called *skinny-dipping,* if I remember correctly.'

With that, she entered her bedroom, shut the door behind her, and they both gave a sigh of relief.

They hurried to the bathroom and washed together so as to feel fresh for bed. Once inside their room, this time, they had no inhibitions about making love in the cottage now that Tina and her mother knew of their relationship. For a while they lay there just enjoying the warmth of each other's bodies as they embraced. They kissed and searched each other's bodies with renewed excitement, wishing to please each other in turn. There was only one doubt that they shared in silence. Tom had to prove to himself that this time he could contain himself long enough to satisfy Bryan and his longing to be taken. The tenderness and care that Bryan showed Tom in his attempt to be the dominant one paid off, for the moment that entry was made, they were able to reach the dizzy heights that they had so longed for. The night seemed endless as they explored and gave erotic thrills to each other with almost their every move. When morning came, they were exhausted but alive with their love for each other. At breakfast they smiled at the attention they were receiving from Tina and mother. The conversation was light yet enquiring, much to the amusement of the two of them. As they walked happily through the tall grasses in the meadow they laughed about the new situation they found themselves in. Once they had reached the river, they stripped themselves of clothing and swam to the willow tree. The sun was now reaching its peak at mid-day and help set the mood for continued love making. Their lovemaking found them rolling on the grass banking and they laughed as Tom mounted Bryan only to find himself sliding on his knees down the banking and back into the water. This routine continued for the rest of the week and was taken light heartedly, leaving the nights in bed to consummate their relationship and where they rotated their roles to suite the mood of the night. Tina had warmed to Tom, and her mother started to treat him as if he were her son. During their time spent relaxing in the garden, they talked of their love for each other trying to rid themselves of the guilt that society imposed on them. How could they get others to understand how same sex partners could find pleasure in their lovemaking?

Lightning Source UK Ltd.
Milton Keynes UK
UKOW04f0616180315

248073UK00001B/115/P